ALL
OF
You

RESCUE ME COLLECTION

LINDSAY DETWILER

HOT TREE
PUBLISHING

All of You © 2018 by Lindsay Detwiler

For information, contact the publisher, Hot Tree Publishing.
WWW.HOTTREEPUBLISHING.COM

EDITING: HOT TREE EDITING
COVER DESIGNER: CLAIRE SMITH
FORMATTER: RMGRAPHX

ISBN-13: 978-1-925655-32-2

10 9 8 7 6 5 4 3 2 1

MORE from Lindsay

To my husband, Chad

Prologue

Alex

I swerved to the side of the road, certain she was gone, the blackness of her hair fluttering behind her and blending into the darkness of the night. Just like so many things in life, one second she was there, hunched into herself under the bright streetlights on the Cedar Bend Bridge, clutching something like it was her lifeblood. And then, in the next second, she was gone, slithered away as if she'd slipped through the cracks of life itself, obliterated from existence.

If I hadn't been driving by, if I hadn't seen her disappear with my own eyes, no one would have noticed her descent into darkness, into the lapping waters of the gentle river, or of her almost goodbye.

But I *was* there. I did see her.

The truth was, looking back, I should've seen her even before the fateful night that tossed our lives together.

I should've seen her in every goodbye I'd said

before her. I should've seen her in every wistful dream I'd walked by and didn't chase. I should've seen her in every empty seat beside me for the twenty-six years I didn't know I was missing her.

She was the lifeblood I waited to uncover. She was the answer to the midnight wish I didn't know I'd asked for. I wouldn't know it until long after I first saw her. I couldn't have known until I met her that I needed her.

Because when I swerved my car to the side of the bridge, chest heaving with adrenaline and fear, I had no idea Marley Jade would eviscerate everything I ever thought I knew about life. I didn't know I would end up saving her that night and on many nights to come.

Most of all, I didn't know she would save me from something I didn't even know I needed saving from.

Chapter One

Alex

I turn the radio down as if this is going to help things, as if a lower volume of Bruno Mars's song will help me not be fifteen minutes late for my shift.

"Shit," I mutter to the hula girl on my dashboard, a memento from the spring break trip my roommates went on without me.

I glance at the clock in my dashboard, each minute that ticks by feeling like the end of my career creeping closer. So much for the solid impression I thought I'd established these past few weeks in the Rosewood ER. How could I be such an idiot? Pretty sure Dr. Conlan isn't going to be too pleased his doctor in residency's late again. The weariness in my bones begs me to turn the car around, to take the break I already desperately need from the crazy hours. The persistent dreamer in me, though, knows I'm too close to my goal to screw things up now. Just a few more years and the white coat will be completely earned, my life path set before me just as I'd planned. I'll have everything I ever dreamed of—if I can just get to the damn hospital.

My Chevy chugging over the now-familiar bridge from my one-bedroom to the hospital, I glance across the barren two lanes of traffic as something on the ledge catches my eye.

I ease up on the gas, although I'm already late and can't afford to.

It's dark, but the streetlight casts an eerie glow over her raven-black hair, long and straight, as it billows in the wind. She's wearing a bright red hat that contrasts with her hair in a way that steals my gaze from the road. I grasp the wheel tighter, reminding myself to pay attention to my driving, snapping away from the call of her. Not like there's much traffic, but it won't do for tonight's ER doctor to end up there himself.

Still, I can't take my eyes off the slumping body on the ledge, her legs bunched up as she clutches them. As I get closer, I notice there's something in her hand, a crinkled bag. She looks shifty and lost, but with an air of beauty I can sense even from behind my grimy windshield.

It's odd, and maybe it's the mixture of energy drinks and Doritos I had for dinner, but it's like I want to know her story. Something about her checked flannel shirt and lace-up boots, the way she's clutching the bag like it's her last possession on earth, makes me want to approach her, to know her.

And then my heart stops, my foot slamming on the brakes.

Because, as if the wind took her into its gripping claws, she's gone, tumbling down, hair wafting behind her in a grand exit that must only be a few seconds but feels like a slow-motion horror scene.

She's over the bridge, and I realize the lost look might not have been imagined.

I'm late for work, but it looks like my work might have come to me, because this girl, whether she meant to or not, has just slipped way too far down for her to walk away unscathed.

***

I swerve to the side of the road, panic dissipating as the doctor in me takes over. I only have a few minutes to get to her before it's too late. The bridge is high but a survivable fall. Still, if she has any sort of lacerations, or hits her head on the way down, all sorts of complications could prevent her from surfacing.

Dashing across the empty street, I quickly peer down over the edge to assess the situation. Seeing nothing but murky water, the streetlights' beams ricocheting off the relatively calm waters, I do the senseless thing, emboldened by my previous summers' job.

I dive in after her.

My dive isn't Olympic-worthy, but it does the trick. My hands cut through the water, a jolt to my system. Now that I'm in here, my clothes dragging me downward, I realize how impulsive my split-second decision was. The girl is nowhere to be seen, and in the chilly night, it seems like an impossible task to find her. I scan the surface, hoping to see even a hint of her rising from the depths of the water.

About ten feet away from me, she emerges, a sputtering, coughing mess. She flounders and flails in the water.

"Stay calm," I yell, swimming over to her hurriedly, wrapping an arm around her, and kicking us both back toward the shore. I'm already tiring from fighting the current, but luckily the water isn't too choppy tonight. It's manageable. Maybe all those summers at the pool paid off after all.

I swim to the shore, the ragged girl in my arms, her black hair drenched and sticking to her face as she continues to gasp for air and spew up water. When I finally get to the bank of the river, I haul us both out in a swift but difficult maneuver, trying to place her on the ground as carefully as I can.

I take a deep breath before the physician-in-training takes over. "I'm Dr. Alex Evans. Can you hear me? Do you know your name?"

She coughs and then gasps, looking like she's trying to catch her bearings, her eyes half-closed.

"Marley," she croaks, looking up into my eyes as I examine her for injuries. The red hat is still miraculously on her head, but I yank it off. I look for contusions or lacerations under the dim glow of the streetlight but don't see any. Glancing over her, checking her eyes, I don't see any immediate damage. Other than being drenching wet, confused, and exhausted, she seems to be okay. There could be underlying damage, though. She'll need to be checked out.

Plus, there's also the consideration of why she fell from the bridge. Was it purposeful? Did some other medical incident happen?

She strains to sit up, but I push her back down. "Stay put. I'm going to call for an ambulance, okay? You stay here while I go get my phone from my car."

Waving a hand in front of her, she says, "I'm fine. I don't need an ambulance. But thank you. Thank you for saving me. I just... I wasn't expecting that. I got all disoriented in the water." Refusing my insistence that she stay still, she props herself up on her elbows, wiping a strand of hair away that is stuck to her face, weariness still evident in her voice and lethargic movements. I can tell, though, she's doing her best to convince me she's okay, her eyes now marked by a defiance that seems to taunt me.

"I really think you should be checked out," I insist, appraising the situation, including a slight trembling of her hands as she reaches for the red hat I've thrown on the bank nearby.

"I like the sound of that," she says, giving me a wink and a smile despite the precarious situation as she shoves the drenched hat onto her sopping wet head. She could've died, but she's here cracking jokes.

Maybe she *is* mentally unstable. I don't smell alcohol on her breath, so I don't think she's drunk.

I don't say a word, just stare.

"Relax, Doctor. It was a joke. I promise I'm okay, and I promise it was an accident. I'm not suicidal if that's what you're thinking. Just having a rough day."

"It was a pretty decent fall. You're lucky."

"I'm something, but lucky usually isn't it," she replies, an odd remark to say the least.

She struggles to stand, and I offer her my hand, yanking her to her feet. Her skin is cold and clammy, and she's shivering. Her voice sounds smoky, perhaps from the situation she's just been through, or maybe it's just partially the quality of her voice. It stirs something in me. Now that the rush of the situation is over and things aren't so critical, I take a second to drink her in. Her clothes, soaked through, stick to her in all the right places, showing off a petite yet womanly frame. She's got an edge to her, from her voice to her clothes, that screams different. But different on her looks good.

Get it together, I tell myself. *This girl could've died and you're checking her out.* Professional.

"So," she says now, wringing out her shirt with her hands. "I'm not sure of the protocol after a doctor dives into the river to save your klutzy ass. Other than thank you, of course. I don't know. Do we exchange numbers? Do I offer to buy you lunch or something?" She grins mischievously.

This girl's different. Very different.

Still, I can't ignore the facts. She allegedly fell from the bridge. She had a brown bag. Maybe this girl's just trouble.

"Look, I'm heading to the ER for my shift. I can't in good conscience let you just walk away like this. It was quite a fall. Will you please at least come with me so we can make sure you're okay?"

We walk up the bank now. I offer her my hand, but she scurries up herself.

"I don't know. I don't really like doctors and hospitals."

I grin.

"No offense," she adds quickly. "Just makes me nervous."

"Well, on a plus side, the doctor in residency is pretty nice. I hear he's handsome, too. And he might even be able to sneak you a cup of coffee, the good stuff, not the ones they have in the vending machine that taste like watered-down tar."

She shifts her eyes to the ground, her smile fading as she considers. For a moment, the lost look is back, the bridge-ledge girl is back. I think she's going to say no.

Instead, she sighs as if in surrender. "Fine. But I'm not staying for a ton of tests, just so you know. I've got work in the morning."

"Deal." We head back to my car, and as she walks to the passenger side, I scramble to toss the stack of fast food bags and empty energy drink cans from the seat. My car's the place where I let it go, where I don't worry about being organized. It's a junk hole, in truth, something I regret now as Marley climbs in.

"Not much of a healthy eater for a doctor," she observes, stepping on an empty can I couldn't reach. She doesn't seem to mind, though, and buckles herself in.

I shrug, slightly embarrassed. "We all have our weaknesses."

"Indeed," she murmurs, turning the knob on the radio to find a station she likes as I buckle up and head toward work.

"Do you have anyone you want to call?" I ask, offering her my phone from the center console.

"Nope. I'm good," she replies with a weak smile I don't quite believe. She's putting on a good show, looking like she's not shaken, trying to seem like she didn't just fall from a bridge into a river where she could've drowned.

So I hit the gas, heading toward Rosewood ER for a lecture from Dr. Conlan, some quick assurances Marley's okay, and some confusion about how life is truly a weird thing.

Chapter Two

Marley

I hug the paper-thin hospital blanket around my shoulders, constricting the cold and the anxiety out of myself. A kind nurse gave me a change of clothes, but the hideous gray sweatpants are about three sizes too big and the T-shirt is my least favorite color—vomit green. Although I'm not sure anyone really likes vomit green.

Dangling my feet over the edge of the hospital bed, I sigh in frustration. I should be at home right now. I should be tucked away in bed, drifting off into dreamland, not sitting here waiting to get an all-clear I know will come. I'm fine.

At least I'm fine from the fall.

Walking out on the Cedar Bend Bridge, crinkled paper sack in my hand, I knew I was making a mistake. I was acting more like the sixteen-year-old Marley instead of the twenty-one-year-old I am. Insolent, impulsive, and moody—these were not the ways to fix problems.

But Mom was out of control again, and I just needed to feel in control. I needed the crisp air in my lungs so I could remember to breathe. I needed nothingness, blackness, peace. Cedar Bend is where I go to find it, sitting on the edge, thinking how easy it would be to fall.

Remembering where so much in my life changed not so long ago, the crinkled paper bag of heartache reminding me it's a choice to stay strong, to stay unbroken.

Tonight, though, my little artsy metaphor failed because I actually did fall. Luckily, though, I'm not completely broken. I survived, thanks to a stoic doctor with seriously sexy looks and a noteworthy set of biceps. I guess if you're going to almost drown in what looks like a suicide attempt, you may as well do it when a man with immense sex appeal is near.

Dammit Marley, calm your hormones, I tell myself, shaking my head. Look at me. I'm not exactly what I'd describe as the doctor's type. Or anyone's type, in reality.

Not that I'm low on self-esteem or drowning in negative feelings about myself. I've prided myself on keeping my body in check, and accepted my quirky looks. Still, a girl with countless tattoos and a biting sense of dark humor isn't what I'd typify as the studious, saving-people type. Looking at him, I can see a little into who he is. The messy car isn't fooling me. This guy's got himself together, his eyes on his goals.

Meanwhile, I work at a coffee bar in a town basically forgotten, my nose ring my most exciting dream realized.

A knock at the door snaps me out of my ruminations. I pull the blanket tighter. I really don't like doctors or medical visits.

"Marley Jade, what the hell are you doing here?" a voice bellows through the door. I smile; the voice belongs to a familiar face.

"Dr. Conlan. I just missed you. Figured I'd throw myself in the river just to get your attention."

He raises an eyebrow, wordlessly telling me my comment isn't amusing.

"Relax. I'm fine. It was an honest mistake. Fell over the ledge."

"And do I even want to ask why you were sitting on the ledge?" he asks, glancing at my chart before he eyes me above his glasses.

I shrug. "It's peaceful."

"Except when you're almost plummeting to your death. Dr. Evans filled me in."

I sigh. "So, he thinks I am suicidal."

"No. He thinks you need to be checked out for head trauma, just to be sure."

"So, he's a worrywart."

"He's thorough. And he's new. Wouldn't do to kill one of the town's best girls in the first few weeks, huh?"

I grin, shaking my head. "Where's this guy from, anyway? I haven't seen him around."

"California. He's been busy settling in and learning the hospital."

I raise an eyebrow. "He's from California, and he came here? To this dinky town?"

"It's not so bad of a town," Dr. Conlan says, his wrinkled hand reaching out to put the stethoscope on my chest. I hate doctors—except Dr. Conlan. He's okay in my books.

"If you're okay with Chick-fil-A's opening five years ago being the biggest excitement in your life. Seriously, he traded California for this place?"

"Not always a choice in residency. You don't always get your first pick. But he said he liked the thought of a small town for his residency. Wanted to check out what things were like in a smaller setting. Believe it or not, we have a decent residency program."

"Oh, I see. He's not here because he wants to be."

"That could always change," Dr. Conlan responds, shining a light into my eyes as he grins.

"What's that supposed to mean?"

"Nothing. Just seems sort of interesting that he found you. Kind of like fate or something."

"Really? You're telling me you're a fate kind of guy?"

"When you've worked this job as long as I have, Marley, you start to believe in things like that. Sometimes that's the only explanation."

I shake my head—once he's done searing my eyeballs out with his bright-as-the-sun light.

"Marley, talk to me. How's your mom? Margaret and I haven't seen her around much."

I exhale, remembering my secrets at home aren't secrets from Dr. Conlan. He's been our neighbor since I was born. He knows more about my life than anyone, for better or worse.

"Not good. Things got rough last night."

"You know our door is always open. Your room is still untouched."

I smile, thinking about the pink walls and the rose-covered comforter Margaret bought for me when I was seven. I'd stayed with Margaret and Joe Conlan quite a few times over the years when Mom wasn't well.

"And I love you guys for it. But I'm okay. I'm not a little girl anymore."

"That doesn't mean you have to be tough all the time, Marley. Just saying."

"Well, my tough skull helped out tonight, didn't it? See, I'm fine. I told you."

"I think you're right. Just please, if you want to impress the new doctor in residency, you don't need to fling yourself off the ledge to do it. Just ask him to go for coffee."

"Joe Conlan. You know I'm not interested in a relationship." I shake my head and turn away from him, grinning in spite of myself.

"Marley Jade, why not? You know, not all men are

the devil. Look at me. I'm not half bad."

I chuckle as he readjusts his glasses. "I agree. You're not half bad." I concur.

He leans in to give me a hug, smiling as I thank him. "See you tomorrow, kid. I'll come check up on you."

"Thanks, Joe. Tell Margaret I'll be over to see her soon."

He turns to leave. "Oh, and Marley? Listen, don't say never because of what happened in your past. Stay open to possibility, you know? There are worse things than falling—in love, that is."

Before I can argue, Joe is out the door, and I'm left with my paper-thin blanket, squeezing myself tighter.

***

At Joe's insistence, I take a taxi home after getting the all-clear. It's probably one of three taxis in the town. Being a taxi driver isn't exactly profitable in a town with about three restaurants and a movie theater for entertainment. When it pulls up to the familiar white house, I realize I don't have any money with me. The driver notices the panic on my face.

"It's fine. Doc Conlan paid for it."

I shake my head. Of course he did. That man thinks of everything.

I thank the driver, close the door, and traipse up the familiar, cracked driveway, plowing through the door that's eternally unlocked. Not like there's much to steal here anyway, and not like anyone in this town would think about robbing this place.

The house is pitch-black, my breathing the only sound. I don't bother flicking on a light to eye up the tower of dishes I know are in the sink, or the random clutter. I feel my way down the hallway like a blind person, tiptoeing until I reach my bedroom door.

When I get there, I launch myself into my bed, the same bed from my childhood days, and wonder how the hell I got here. I stare at the ceiling, the crazy night swirling in my head like a nausea-inducing carnival ride. The screaming match with Mom. The slamming door. The snap in me. The crumpled bag, almost giving in to temptation.

The fall.

The rescue.

Alex.

As I close my eyes and let sleep take over, I think about how shitty things are, how it's messed up that I'm still here, always right here, in the same broken-down house with the same broken-down life.

Above all, I think about how shitty it is I couldn't even hold on to that.

***

The alarm's infernal blare comes too soon. I feel like hell the next morning, the chipper Samba music infuriating me like it always does. I've never been a morning person. I slap at my phone before groaning and sitting up to figure out how to shut the damn music off. After fumbling with way too many buttons,

I manage to silence what might as well be a funeral dirge. I rub the sleep from my eyes as I drag myself out of bed.

Another day.

After a five-minute shower and the realization we're out of hair conditioner, I toss my wet hair into a bun, throw on some clothes that will pass for work, and saunter out the door, glad I have a ten-minute walk to get awake.

The sun beams down on me, a contrast to my dark mood. I try to shrug it off. It's a new day. There's no use dwelling on the messed-up situation last night. I'm usually much better at smiling through.

As soon as I walk in the door at work, Becca comes rushing toward me, her flouncy blonde ponytail swinging.

"Oh my God, Marley, are you okay? Dane just told me what happened. You shouldn't be here. You should be resting. You could have died!"

I stare at Becca, thankful there are only a few elderly patrons in the corner of the shop. I shake my head, Becca's words rattling through me at a mile a minute. Apparently, she's already made herself her customary three lattes this morning.

"Becca, I'm fine. Really. It wasn't a big deal."

"Not a big deal? Mom said you could've drowned," Dane says, coming up behind her.

Dane owns Georgia's, Rosewood's finest organic coffee bar—named after his mother, who is a nurse at

Rosewood Hospital. He's more than my boss, though. He's truly become a friend over the years. Even though we went to high school together, we were never close back then. He was the straight-A student; I was the girl smoking in the bathroom, skipping class, and barely passing. He was the cocky jock who told everyone my name was Bob Marley and harassed me whenever he got the chance.

The harassment part still hasn't quite changed. Neither has his penchant for success.

Perhaps this is why at nineteen, Dane opened Georgia's, and I ended up pouring coffee for him. And never left.

I know it could be worse. I'm thankful to have a job that helps pay the bills and is mostly pleasant— Becca's excessive perkiness aside.

"That's right, Marley. Drowned. As in D-R-O-W-N-E-D."

I shake my head. You've got it. Becca was a cheerleader in high school. She graduated one year after me. And, as you probably already guessed by now, she also wasn't one of my close friends. The bouncy cheerleader doesn't usually make time for the Poe-loving, tattoo-sporting rebel of the school.

It's funny, though, because a few years out of high school and, other than her perky, cheer-like spellings of potentially deadly situations, you'd forget we were in different cliques. Getting to know her these past few years, I've realized she isn't half bad.

If you can deal with her incessant glee, that is.

"I'm fine, really. It was an accident."

"Well, Mom did tell me the new doctor saved you. And she also told me he's quite easy on the eyes," Dane says, elbowing me in the ribs. His mother is both the head ER nurse and the town's biggest gossip.

Of course, in a town as small as Rosewood, forgetting to get your newspaper in the morning makes its rounds in the gossip circles. You can't do anything in peace here, let alone fall off a bridge.

"Everyone's being a bit dramatic. It's all good." I grab my apron and tie it around my waist, trying to ignore the hovering coworkers who are definitely invading my personal space this morning.

"So, is it true? Is he sexy?" Becca asks as she follows me behind the counter.

"I don't know. Go check him out if you're so curious," I respond with a bit of edge in my voice.

I put on my name tag, trying not to stab myself like I normally do, as Becca and Dane simultaneously say, "He must be hot."

I sigh, heading to the back to get some cupcakes and cookies to restock the front display. The morning rush is about to begin, and I'm ready to put all this crazy talk behind me. I'm ready to blend back in, to be Marley the brooding barista who is just sort of standing still.

Becca animatedly moves on from the depressing talk of my almost death and starts chatting about college and new roommates and the psychology class that is just to die for—she seriously says that.

I smile and nod at the appropriate times, truly glad to see her so happy. She's a good person, she really is.

But I can't help but feel a little bit of envy creeping in.

I know it's my fault. I know the position I'm in is because of the choices I've made. There is no excuse for what I've done to my life, no matter what anyone says. I could've decided to rise above it all. I didn't. Instead, I submerged myself in rebellion while my mother drowned herself in sorrow and the bottle. By the time I realized what I was doing, it was too late.

So here I am, wiping counters, measuring coffee beans, and listening to the same chatter from the elderly patrons, the business professionals, and the college freshmen who swing by Georgia's. I'm stuck staring at the latte machine, wondering how long changing the daily specials sign out front will be my biggest excitement.

All around me, it seems like everyone's moving on. Dane's got this place, but he's looking to buy another coffee franchise, too, and expand his business. Becca's going back to college in New York in a few weeks.

It'll just be me and Louise, the elderly lady Dane hired who barely makes eye contact with me other than to glower.

Despite Becca's laughter and the warm sunshine streaming through the front window, I can't channel

21

any Bob Marley—my mother loves him, hence my name—and let it all go.

I make it through the morning rush in a daze, pouring more coffees than I can count before it's finally time for a break.

I head outside to my only sanctuary, my only sanity in this standstill life, my turquoise journal in hand as I venture out into the familiarity of Rosewood and the reprieve of my saving grace.

***

Despite the sun's warmth, my favorite beanie adorns my head. At this point, it's become my thing. I feel naked without it.

Sitting under my favorite umbrella on the patio at Georgia's, I crack open the journal and read yesterday's musings. Good thing I wrote them in the morning before the paper bag, Humpty Dumpty wall incident. They may have been a little gloomier otherwise.

I read my work about the tree, my favorite tree, and nod, a little impressed by myself. It's not perfect, but it's not too bad, either.

I flip the page, ready to put pen to paper, ready to go into the trance I've welcomed since childhood. When the screaming got too loud, when the worries became too dark, this is where I escaped.

This is still my escape, the soft words taking the edge off life.

"Hey, Marley, how are you feeling?" a voice asks

from behind me. I recognize the voice, but my mind doesn't quite place it, not here.

I turn to see Alex. He's wearing scrubs, his white coat, and he's sporting some pretty noticeable dark circles.

Still, he looks damn good in that coat, especially with stubble defining his already strong jawline. There's something about a man in uniform and all that.

I shake my head as if I can shake loose the lascivious thoughts building within.

"Hey, I'm fine," I say, not sure how to respond. I didn't expect him here.

"I'm glad. Dr. Conlan said you were all clear last night. Pretty lucky, I guess."

I grin. "Yeah, this pretty decent guy helped me out. He's not too shabby, you know?"

"I've heard he's got some good biceps going," he jokes, flexing and then shaking his head, laughing at his ridiculous pose. On some men, it would seem arrogant. On him, with his reddening face marked by dimples, it's charming. I can tell he doesn't take himself too seriously—at least when it comes to his muscles.

"So, what are you doing? Off to work?" I ask, trying my hand at small talk.

Alex shakes his head. "Just heading home."

My jaw drops. "Wait, you haven't been home yet? You just got off your shift?"

"Uh-huh. Hence the need for a coffee IV at this point."

I shake my head. "I'm going to have to have a word

with Joe. Working you to death over there. Oops, bad pun I guess."

"It's fine. I don't mind it. The work I mean, not the pun. I've been learning a lot."

"You know, now that I think about it… he didn't send you to check up on me, did he?" I ask, raising an eyebrow.

Alex puts up a hand, shaking his head. "No, no. I promise I'm not stalking you. Dr. Conlan just said this was the best coffee shop in town."

"Sure he did," I add, smiling. That Joe is sly. He knows I always work this shift Tuesdays.

"Is it a lie? Should I go somewhere else?"

"No, it *is* the best coffee in town. I just suspect Joe had other motives."

"Like what?" He grins to look innocent, but I can tell from his face he knows exactly what I mean.

"Never mind. Just follow me. I'll get you a cup on the house. Newcomers' special."

I stand from my seat, grabbing my journal.

"I don't want to interrupt," Alex states, gesturing toward my journal in my hand.

"It's fine. Break will be over soon enough. I'll write later."

"So you're a writer?" he asks as I lead him through the door.

I feel my cheeks warm. "Not really. Just as a hobby."

"What do you like to write?"

"Poetry."

"That's awesome. Can I read something?"

I stare at him like he's got three heads. He puts a hand up again.

"Sorry. Didn't mean to overstep. I just have never really known a poet before."

I smile now. "I'm not *really* a poet."

"And how do you know it?" Alex asks, and then smirks. "Sorry, couldn't resist."

I roll my eyes, but the smile spreads as I readjust my beanie. "Oh my Lord, you must be sleep deprived. That was terrible."

"You're right. On both accounts."

I lead Alex to the counter. Becca and Dane turn to me, then do a double take.

"Oh my, he is definitely a looker," Becca "whispers." In actuality, the girl doesn't know what a whisper is, so it's more like a shout.

Alex turns an even darker shade of red.

"So, how do you like it?" I ask, trying to distract Alex from the awkward situation. The poor guy doesn't look like the type to handle being the center of attention, especially in a small coffee shop he's just walked into.

"I bet he likes it all kinds of ways," Dane murmurs, elbowing Becca, and the two grin.

Now it's my turn to blush even more. I'm not sure why; it's not like I said it. Still, I find myself turning to Alex and apologizing.

"Sorry, Alex. They're so backward they don't know

how a true place of business is run."

Alex just shrugs, his face still painted with a smile. "I'll just drink it black."

"Black? Really?" I question.

"What's wrong with that?"

I shrug before replying, "Nothing. Just that I read an article that psychopaths are more likely to drink black coffee."

"Okay, surprise me then."

"No, no, we aim to please here," I retort, pouring his coffee into the foam cup with Georgia's logo on it. Becca snorts a little, and I roll my eyes. "Okay, really? Are we in high school again? Are you two going to turn everything into an innuendo? Can you please grow up?"

Becca and Dane look at each other before Dane says, "That's no fun."

I sigh. "You're kind of right. But anyway, Alex, please don't judge Georgia's by the customer service or lack thereof. The coffee is amazing. Seriously."

"So how long have you worked here?" Alex asks me.

"Since it opened. So two years."

He nods as I hand him the to-go cup of coffee. I added a little bit of half-and-half to make me feel better about the psychopath possibility.

Mercifully, the phone rings, and Dane goes to answer it as a customer walks through the door. Becca busies herself with Greg, her latest crush, adding an extra ponytail twirl for good measure.

"It seems like a great place to work."

"It is. Even though they drive me crazy sometimes, the people are awesome."

"Seems like a nice town overall," he says, leaning on the counter as I tidy up, feeling the need to keep my hands busy.

"Yeah. Pretty low-key. I'm sure it's lame compared to where you're from."

"Not lame. But definitely more low-key. I like it though. It's a nice change of pace."

I stare at this man before me, a man who has probably seen more of the world than I could ever dream of. A man who is going places, who has been places.

It's like I'm staring at someone from another world.

"Well, I better let you get going so you can get some sleep," I comment, not sure what else to talk about. I don't know why I feel so flustered around him.

"Yeah, I need to catch a few hours before I need to be back."

"Wait, you have to be back in a few hours? Seriously?"

"No rest for the weary, I guess."

"Do you get *any* time off?"

He looks like he's mentally ticking off his schedule. "Thursday. I'm off all day Thursday."

"Well, what do you know? Marley's short shift this week is Thursday. Imagine that," Dane pipes in, apparently done with his phone call already.

"No, it's not. I work all day," I argue.

"Not anymore. Becca asked for extra hours that day, so I switched your schedule. You only work eight to noon. Imagine that," he declares, winking at me.

I exhale.

Alex stares at me, seeming to size up my reaction. "So, any plans after work then?"

I shrug. "Binge watching *The Bachelor* and napping. My go-to."

"Any chance you might be able to spare a few hours to show a new guy around? I still feel a little lost around here, like an outsider. It'd be good to get a tour of the local haunts."

The fluttering feeling returns, and I fiddle with the stack of foam cups nearby. *Is he asking me out?*

Obviously not. The guy's probably still worried about my mental state after the whole bridge situation. He probably has me on suicide watch or as a case study.

Regardless, I decide *The Bachelor* can wait. Life's about living in the moment, I remind myself. Life's about seizing opportunities. I need to start doing that.

Not that showing a man I barely know around this dinky town is a life-changing opportunity. Still, it's something. It beats hours on the couch in scruffy sweatpants stuffing my face with ice cream.

So I lift my shoulder. "Okay. Sure."

He beams. "I'll pick you up here after your shift? Is that okay?"

"Sounds great."

Alex takes a sip of his coffee. "Damn, that's good. I think Dr. Conlan was right. Best cup of coffee I've ever had."

"Something tells me you'll be back for more," Dane says, now winking at Alex.

"Can you not be so creepy?" I ask, shaking my head but smiling.

"Wait, you own the place?" Alex inquires.

"I know. Hard to believe, huh?" I add.

"Well, I think it's great."

"And I've got some pretty great employees, too, right? Clumsy employees apparently, but great," Dane says, and Alex smiles.

"See you Thursday, Marley. Thanks for the coffee." Alex holds his cup of coffee up as if he's toasting me. It's weird but also kind of cute.

"My pleasure," I respond, smiling awkwardly until he leaves Georgia's, the bells tinkling as the door closes behind him.

"My pleasure?" Dane questions. "What is this, the 1950s?"

"I don't do this sort of thing, okay?" I add, frustrated.

"What sort of thing?" Becca pipes up, Greg having left to go to work.

"I don't know. This. Guy thing."

"Uh-oh," Dane singsongs. "Someone's falling in more ways than one, looks like."

"Stop. I'm not. I'm just being nice to the guy who saved my life."

"Yeah, I'd believe it if you weren't so fidgety. I've only seen you like this one other time," Becca adds, smiling, clapping her hands. "Oh, you're in love. L-O-V-E, love."

I groan. "Stop it, you two. Why is everyone conspiring for me to be with someone?"

Dane's face falls a little, and he grows serious. "Because, honey, you deserve it. You deserve to let some love in. Seriously."

I inhale, turning to look out the window at the sunny day, wondering if he's right.

Wondering if it's finally my turn to find happiness, the happiness I didn't think was truly possible for me.

Chapter Three

Marley

I take the long way home, stopping underneath my favorite oak to scrawl some more ideas in my journal, the slightly damp grass not bothering me enough to make me get up once I've sat down. I sit for a long time, the sun slowly fading into the horizon as I lean my head back on the familiar trunk. Scratching down words and phrases from the day, I try to make some sense of them.

I jot down Alex's name in my journal like some sad sixth grader writing her crush's name on her folder in gel pen. I draw question marks around his name and find myself smiling.

Alex.

The doctor who saved my life, although that sounds a bit melodramatic, even for an aspiring poet.

But he did. He saved me. Not just from the waters of the river, either. He saved me from my gloom and doom, from the pit of despair I was wallowing in last night on the bridge.

My eyes dance over the purple wildflower growing near the tree, my favorite. Now, I'm showing him around our quiet town. What does this mean? Could this be the change I've been waiting for?

Not that I haven't dated. There were quite a few flings in my late teens, perhaps my wily heart thinking love was what I was searching for. But looking back, love didn't describe the lascivious looks and the wham-bam nights of passion. It was something more carnal, but not eternal.

Love wasn't what I'd felt, and I don't know if love is even what I need now.

Love, lust, or maybe just a friendly town tour, I do know one thing. That man's hands are firm and strong, just the way I like them. His muscles aren't bad either.

Most of all, he's got the kind of eyes I could stare into for days. Not just a nice color, either. No, he's got eyes that seem to bare his soul, that seem to say he's got depth and heart and character.

I barely know him, in truth. Still, he doesn't quite seem like the kind of guy I would fall for. He's very different from my motorcycle-mayhem badass boyfriend at nineteen. He's nothing like my first love, Noah, who ended up on the run for arson. He doesn't seem like any of them at all.

Alex doesn't appear to be the kind of guy to live life on the edge or to indulge in the free-roaming kind of life. He's rigid and stoic. He's straitlaced and serious.

He's everything I'd never imagine my heart fluttering for.

But it did. From the moment he pulled me out of the river and turned all doctor-like on me, I was entranced.

Not that it means anything, I remind myself. He's just new here. Pretty sure a bridge-sitting, lace-up boots kind of girl like me isn't quite what he's looking for. I'm more of a Wednesday Adams person, while he seems to be more like a Ward Cleaver. A very sexy, tempting Ward Cleaver, at that.

Not that I'm judging.

Okay, I'm judging

Why are you overanalyzing this? I ask myself, gently bumping the back of my head against the tree trunk. It's not like this is going anywhere. The guy drew the short straw in residency placements, and he'll be out of here in a few years—if he doesn't die of boredom in this sleepy town before then.

Don't get me wrong. Rosewood isn't a horrible place. It's just the kind of place where a new supermarket is front page news and a dead rosebush in Mrs. Fillibell's garden is morning gossip.

I'm sure even an organized, color-inside-the-lines kind of guy like Alex will feel this place falls a little short on the excitement meter.

Glancing down at my journal, I shake off all thoughts of Alex. This isn't a big deal. I'm just overly interested because it's a fresh face in a town where I know everyone too well, and I've gone through the decent and not-so-decent stock of guys. I'm apparently craving change in any form.

I put pen to paper after flipping the page, determined to leave the Alex and the question marks behind. I start scribbling down words, looking up at the sky now and then to clear my head, to urge the words to flow.

Mostly, though, I sit and stare, doodling random squiggles in the margins of the lined paper and thinking about today, last night, and my entire life.

What am I doing?

It's a question I've asked so many times but never seem to answer.

What am I doing with my life? What am I doing here in Rosewood?

There used to be a time when, despite everything, I thought I could find happiness. I would look at pictures of Paris and Belize and Shanghai and light up at the thought of traveling there, of seeing, of living. I used to sit in my room, drowning out Mom's midnight rants with travel videos on YouTube, making a list of all the places I would go. I had no idea what I wanted to do or how I would get to all the places on my list—but that wasn't the point. The point was I knew even at fifteen there was so much more out there, so much to see and live. I wanted to do it all. I thought maybe by some miracle things would change, and that I'd get my chance.

Even then, I think a part of me knew the lure of the dream was that it wouldn't happen. I'd be lucky to see the next county, let alone another country. My grades were abysmal, we didn't have any money, and even if those things weren't true, I didn't think I could do it. I couldn't leave her, no matter what.

And even then, I knew she'd never change. She couldn't.

She's all I have, all I have left besides Joe and Margaret, of course, who pushed me to do better, to think ahead, and to dream. I just never told them the real reason I wouldn't leave for college, even when they kindly offered to loan me the money I needed. I didn't tell them it wasn't financial or even about not wanting to go.

It was guilt.

I look down, realizing I've drawn a whole lot of black squares. Like so many other things, this poem hasn't gone anywhere.

I didn't pay much attention in school, but I paid enough attention to know they never covered how you go about dealing with it when you wake up at twenty-one and realize you're stuck in a life you didn't dream of. They didn't teach us how to deal with the guilt of wanting to get out of this place and seize life, but not wanting to leave your family behind.

Maybe it's Alex. Maybe it's the bridge. Maybe it's my sort of near-death. Regardless, it's like my mind won't stop wrapping itself around the fear that I'm living all wrong, and life is just slipping through my fingers just like it did for Dad.

"Stop it, Marley," I tell myself, and then glance around to make sure no one is near. The town's already whispering about my potential suicide attempt. I don't need them hearing me talk to myself, or they'll lock me up for sure.

I know life could always be worse. I have a lot to be thankful for. I have a job I don't hate, even if it isn't exactly what I had in mind. I have amazing neighbors, the Conlans, who've been like grandparents to me since I was little. I have a quiet neighborhood, food on the table most days, and clothes on my back.

Life's about perspective, and I've tried to choose to see it with rosy glasses, even when it doesn't feel like I should.

Still, there's something tough about feeling like there's no choice, no way out, no decisions. I feel trapped on a merry-go-round I didn't buy a ticket for but can't get off.

Standing from the ground, wiping the clumps of wet grass from my ass before readjusting my trustworthy hat, I close my journal and traipse home, to the only life I've known and probably ever will.

Chapter Four

Alex

In truth, the coffee's just okay. A little weaker than I like, and not quite my favorite cup from back home. Nonetheless, it tastes pretty good, partially because of the sheer exhaustion taking hold of me.

And, if I'm being honest, in part because of the barista who served it.

I remind myself not to get ahead of myself. I barely know this girl other than our first sketchy and scary encounter. Dr. Conlan certainly sings her praises, and my heart doesn't let up when I'm around her. There's something about her, from the first moment I saw her sitting on that ledge, that screams intriguing.

Captivating or not, though, I don't have time for this. I can't lose focus now, not when I'm so close. I didn't break up with Stacie for no reason. There's no room in my life for love or dating. I have to get this right. I can't mess up now. I've got to keep my eye on the end game.

So why the hell did I ask Marley to show me around? Why did I invite her into my life knowing this can't go anywhere?

I shake my head at my own stupidity. Exhaustion. It must've been sheer exhaustion.

Seems to be my excuse for everything these days.

Or maybe it was because I was thinking with my dick instead of my heart, thinking of the way those skinny black pants clung to her curves as she led me into Georgia's, the way her lips parted just a bit when she poured the coffee.

Maybe it's just a primal instinct surfacing that I've tried to squash for too long.

Or maybe it's because she's a breath of fresh air in a town too small for its own good. Marley, even though Dr. Conlan said she's lived here her whole life, doesn't scream small-town monotony. From her clothes to her mannerisms, she screams worldly. Excitement.

And God knows excitement isn't in my vocabulary, other than medical emergencies, of course.

Walking into my apartment, I sigh, taking my shoes off at the door and wanting nothing more than to sink into bed for a few hours. I set my coffee on the counter beside the bills I need to mail and head to the shower, ready to strip off work before work starts again all too soon.

The steamy water heavenly against my skin, I inhale deeply, leaning against the shower wall, the prospect of scrubbing my hair too much at this point. These hours are insane. Any normal person would want to walk away, no matter how close they were.

But I can't. I'm so close to the success I've been craving, I can taste it. I just have to keep moving. All those hours of studying, those years of locking myself in the library day in and day out are going to pay off.

I'm going to finally make it, finally reach the golden dream I've been chasing since I was fourteen.

I'm finally going to be the man he always thought I would be. I'm going to make him proud.

As I climb into bed, pulling back my Star Wars comforter, I take off the cross necklace my parents gave me when I graduated. It was my grandfather's, also a doctor. Our family heirloom is, I suppose, my good luck charm—hasn't let me down yet. I carefully set it on the nightstand before rolling back onto the pillow, readjusting my boxers, and settling in.

Looking at the relic of the past sitting on the bare white stand, I smile as I doze off.

It's worth it. It's all worth it.

***

The next few days pass in a blur of emergencies, work, espresso, and yawns. I spend most of the next forty-eight hours in the inner core of the hospital, assuaging fears and rushing to stop the bleeding. With Dr. Conlan, I tackle a broken leg, a minor surgical procedure, and five cases of the flu. Even in the smallest town, the ER is never dull.

When I'm not working, I'm either tucked away in my bed sleeping or tucked away on my couch studying medical reference books and researching online. I've learned you can never be done learning in this job. There's always more to discover, and you never know when a piece of information is going to be vital to saving a life.

Still, Wednesday night, looking around my bare apartment that houses only a handful of family photographs and a poster of John Wayne—an obsession in my family, albeit an odd one—I feel a little sad, a bit lonely.

Day in and day out, it's work until exhaustion and then come home to emptiness. My life, although successful in many ways, is also positively lonely.

I'm alone. I'm becoming a hermit.

Correction. I think I'm already there.

So when Thursday rolls around, my day off, I'm glad I made plans with Marley.

It doesn't have to be a torrid romantic affair. It doesn't need to go anywhere. It'll just be good to get out of my man cave—aka apartment—and to get out of the textbooks. It'll be good to look around this town I'm going to call home for quite a while.

And it'll be good to interact with someone who isn't bleeding out or in a life or death situation—at least I hope not. Our track record isn't exactly promising.

I spend a little extra time on Thursday choosing a

ALL OF *You*

clean T-shirt, slapping on some cologne, and shaving.

Strolling down Plum Street and turning onto Main, I realize I'm walking fast even though I've only slept a few hours. Something about today gets my feet moving. Maybe it's the extra dose of vitamin D I'm getting. Lately, I've been feeling a little bit vampire-like.

Maybe, though, it's knowing I'll be seeing her again, my odd night shift hours keeping me from Georgia's since the day I made plans with her. Hopefully she didn't forget.

It's the first day I've had off since I got to Rosewood, and I thought I'd be spending the day sleeping or maybe playing an hour or so of Xbox before studying my rare diseases textbook. Instead, I'm heading out for an adventure with a girl I met on a bridge.

Correction. A girl I met under a bridge in the water.

I feel a little bit weird about it, like there's something unsettling about going out with the girl I saved from drowning.

"Marley's a great girl, trust me," Dr. Conlan had assured me when I mentioned she'd be showing me around today.

"She seems like it."

"Rough times, that girl. But she's risen above it all. She's a good thing, Alex. Good for a guy like you to have a girl like her and vice versa."

I'd nonchalantly nodded, not wanting Dr. Conlan

to think I was being overeager or stalkerish. Secretly, though, I was clinging to every word, happy to know more about the brooding girl who just is still such a mystery.

When Georgia's comes into view, I take a deep breath. I feel oddly nervous, a little unsure.

It's not a date. Get it together, man, I tell myself. This is just Marley being nice, showing me the small-town kindness.

But no matter how much I've told myself nothing is happening between us—that we just met and I don't know this girl—I can't stop thinking about her black hair, perfectly pale skin, and pink lips.

I can't stop thinking about the glimmer of a smile I got to see on her face or the way her eyes light up when she talks. I can't stop admiring the perfect mixture of brooding and sass, of extrovert and introvert.

Still, there's a mystery to her, too. Underneath her crocheted hat, there's something hiding there, something deeper.

Maybe even something darker.

A girl like Marley—from what I know of her at least—isn't the typical girl I go for.

She doesn't seem like the pretty in pink with pearls on the weekends kind of girl. She's not the dainty sips of tea and kale salad, or the I'll have tea instead of soda, and I only drink red wine kind of girl.

These are the girls of my past.

But there was always something missing, I remind

myself. There was always something in the back of my mind that said there was more to life, there was more to love than those innocent pecks on the cheek, those careful lovemaking sessions never talked about later, those perfect girls with it all together. In truth, medical school was the perfect excuse to leave it behind, to stop trying, and to give up on the L-word I'd come to avoid.

But, deep down, there was always a part of me wondering if the girl who could unlock my heart was out there. All along, there was something missing with the kale girls. I just hadn't known what. Looking at Marley, though, as she stands before me in front of Georgia's, her sunshine-yellow sundress pulling my gaze toward her, there's just something different. She doesn't seem like the "perfect pearls, sip a hot tea, careful strolls in the park" kind of girl.

She seems like hell on wheels, her black Converse sneakers and bold vintage necklace contrasting starkly with her feminine, curvy dress. And of course, the hat's on her head.

She's dressed in ways most women her age wouldn't dream of, but on her, it looks comfy. She looks right.

"So you ready for an adventure? You ready to see what this town has to offer?" she asks, those eyes gleaming at me.

"Let's do it," I say, excited for the first time since coming here about what this town could hold for me.

***

"So this is what you call fun?" I ask, panting from the uphill climb. I'm not in terrible shape, although med school hasn't allowed much time for lifting weights or hitting the gym. But this is taking everything out of me.

"It's beautiful, isn't it? Plus, the view at the top is worth it," Marley responds, ahead of me by a few steps, goading me on like I'm some sad pony who needs reassurance.

As I look up at the rest of the hill, I wish to God I had a small pony to pull myself the rest of the way up. I remind myself to play it cool, trying to suppress my huffy breaths and hide the fact my forehead is beading with sweat.

Marley is breathing heavy too, shoving her black hair from her eyes. We plod on, me wondering why the hell I sacrificed my day off to go get sweaty and exhausted.

But looking at the woman in front of me, the dress now sticking to her from sweat, I don't wonder long.

Dammit, she's gorgeous.

"You're not staring at my ass, are you, Doctor?" she says, turning to grin at me. I can't help but notice she sashays just a little bit as she speaks, as if she knows that's exactly what I've been doing.

Not wanting to come off as a creep, I just shake my head, pointing to myself. "Me? Of course not. Just making sure you have good posture so you don't pull a muscle or something."

"I think if anyone's pulling a muscle, it's you. Come on, isn't a doctor supposed to be in good shape?"

"You sure have a lot of stereotypes, huh?"

Marley shrugs. "Well, I've never really gone hiking with a doctor before, so this is new to me."

"And I've never gone on a hellish hike like this. Remind me next time, I'll make the plans."

"Not a chance. I'm the tour guide, remember?" she responds, giving me a coy wink before turning around. "Now stop complaining. We're almost there."

I take some breaths for motivation and trudge upward, reminding myself I can handle it.

When we get to the top, I keel over on a rock to catch my breath. Marley, though, doesn't waste a second. "Come on, take a look. Rosewood in all its glory."

Marley grabs my hand, and I feel a rush. Her warm skin is so soft to the touch, and I can't help but notice my hand fits perfectly around hers.

Her excitement is contagious. She acts like she's never seen this place before. She pulls me to the edge of a treacherous precipice, and I look down.

The sleepy town of Rosewood doesn't look so sleepy up here. It looks soothing and inviting. It looks right.

"Beautiful, huh?" she asks.

"Beautiful," I say, but I'm not looking at Rosewood anymore. I'm gazing at those pink lips that seem to be inviting me in. I'm staring at the perfect curve of her neck, the pale skin accentuating the innocence of it.

I need to get a grip. I'm never like this. Sure, I notice a hot girl when I see her. But this is ridiculous. I'm acting like I've never seen a woman before.

Still, her hand is clutching mine, and it's like it's the most natural thing in the world. Marley leans in on my arm.

"What's it like? California, I mean?" she asks, and I look down at her, the top of her hat underneath my chin.

"Busy. Hectic. But fun. You've never been?"

She just gives a little laugh. "Are you kidding? I've never been out of this state, let alone to California."

"Are you serious?" I question, sure she must be kidding.

"Nope. It was a complicated thing growing up." I can tell by the tone of her voice this is too much to talk about just yet. The girl who seems open to everything is definitely not open to this.

"So are you planning on getting out of here eventually? Traveling? You seem like the type of woman who would have a touch of wanderlust."

"Do I have that look about me?"

I shrug. "It was just a hunch. You have that quality about you."

"And what quality is that?" she probes, regarding me with a smile. I can tell I got at least a part of her right on the dot.

I think for a long moment, not quite sure myself. Finally, I settle on one word. "Free."

Again, she just sort of chuckles, shaking her head. "Hardly. But thank you. I'll take it as a compliment. And to answer your question, not really any plans. Life's just sort of got me stuck right now. Have I thought about it? You bet. But thinking about it and doing it are very different things, you know?"

I nod. "It can be scary. Moving here from the West Coast wasn't exactly what I had planned. But sometimes scary can be good."

"So you're happy here?"

"I mean, it's only been a few weeks, but yeah. It seems like a nice place."

"It is. Small and a little lame. But it's nice. There are good people here," she adds, leaning on my shoulder.

It should be awkward, standing here alone with a girl I barely know. But it isn't. There's something about Marley that is just so easy. All the high-maintenance, don't say the wrong thing kind of relationships I've had in the past seem so foreign compared to this, just the two of us standing here, taking in the quiet scene and talking about dreams.

I breathe in, realizing this is just what I needed. Fresh air, quiet, and companionship—easy, straightforward companionship.

In the midst of my silent meditation, something splatters on my face.

I think I'm imagining it, hallucinations from lack of sleep finally kicking in. But then there's another. And another.

I turn to look at Marley just in time for the rain to start falling steadily, the clouds overhead finally giving way.

The rain quickly turns to a downpour. I put my arms up to shield myself, as if this is going to work.

"Shit. We should get going," I say, turning to head down the trail, expecting Marley to shriek and cover her head, too.

Instead, she just laughs. "Why? Are you the Wicked Witch or something? Are you going to melt?"

She lets go of my hand and stretches her arms out, her face raised to the sky as she smiles, breathing in, laughing a little. "It feels so good."

I stare at her, this mysterious girl in a sunshine-yellow dress acting as if the deluge of rain is a religious rite.

"I take it you like rain?" I ask, my clothes becoming heavy with the soaking downpour.

"Yeah, don't you?" she questions, turning to me as her smile widens. "The only thing better is lightning. I love a good storm. Is that strange?"

I think about it. *Yeah, probably.* "No," I lie.

"You're lying. You think it's weird," she says, still laughing, her dress now soaked through, her hair sticking to her face.

"Okay, it's a little weird."

"There's nothing wrong with a little rain. There are worse things in life."

"This is true," I agree, still feeling like we should be

running for cover, but following Marley's lead and just letting myself get soaked.

"So, Doctor, you ready for our next adventure?" she shouts over the rain.

I grin. "There's more?"

"I told you I was showing you the town highlights. We might be a small town, but we've got more than a hiking trail. From the looks of your car the other night, you're not one of those health nut, kale salad kinds of guy, are you?"

I smile as she looks up at me, one hand on her hip now.

"I mean, I don't have anything against kale." Other than the fact all my exes loved kale and I found it annoying. And disgusting.

"Do you have anything against greasy food with millions of calories that will clog your arteries?"

"Is this a trick question? Are you spying for Dr. Conlan?"

She raises an eyebrow at me. "You never know. But if he were going to hire a spy, he'd probably do a better job. I'm terrible at keeping secrets."

"I'll keep that in mind. But no, I don't have anything against artery-clogging foods, at least on my day off." It was the truth. In reality, the food in my fridge right now is damn embarrassing—beer, lunch meat, and some ketchup. That's about it. Bachelor life is heightened by doctor life, not lending itself to a very healthy meal-making situation at home.

"Good. Let's go, then. I'm going to show you one of the best secrets in Rosewood that only the true locals know about."

I take one last glance at the town I now call home before Marley pulls me down the trail. "Come on, the day's fading away. We have places to go, things to see."

The girl in the sunshine-yellow dress pulls me forward, and I can't help but follow.

***

By the time we get to the bottom of the hike, our feet sloshing in mud on the way down and our clothes drenched, the sun peeks out of the clouds again. I wring out my shirt at the bottom and shake out the water from my hair.

Marley wrings out her dress, and I try not to stare as a sliver of her thigh creeps out.

"That was fun," she says, laughing as she runs a hand through the ends of her hair.

She leads me back to the main part of the park we were in, out the front entrance, and a few blocks toward the center of town.

"Do you want to go change before we go wherever we're going?" I ask. We look like two scraggly, lost people.

"Nah, it's fine," she assures me, waving a hand. "Moe won't care."

"Who's Moe?"

"Just the best damn chef in town."

"The million-calorie food man?" I question.

"And then some," she replies, leading me forward.

We wander down the street, the silence between us hardly awkward. Marley says hi to a few people working in storefronts or passing by. We finally get to our apparent location—a tiny corner restaurant with a broken-down sign. The door's green paint is peeling off in huge strips, and the windows are murky and hazy. It doesn't look like a place I'd ever venture into back home.

Marley bounces through the door, waving to an elderly man behind the counter.

"Moe, we'll take two of the house specials. Dr. Evans here is new."

"Did you say doctor?" Moe says, smiling. "I don't know if my cheesesteaks are doctor-approved."

"He's off duty today so he won't judge your calorie count," Marley adds, leading me to a corner booth. There are a few other couples sitting in the booths and a few elderly guys chatting at the table.

But that's it. It's just Moe, a grill behind him, and a cash register.

"Doesn't Moe have any staff?" I whisper, leaning into Marley.

Marley smiles. "Moe's wife died five years ago. She was his waitress. He refuses to get any help. Says no one can replace Dorothy. Says he doesn't want anyone to try. So he just runs the place by himself now. The cook, the waiter, and the cashier. Food takes a bit to get, but it's worth it. Trust me."

"I'm in no hurry," I state, staring straight at her.

"Good. But we do have a few more places to see."

"Such as?"

"Well, we've got our own roller skating rink, believe it or not. We've also got the lucky statue of Mr. Rosewood, the founder of the town. Legend says if you get a selfie with the statue, you have a year of good luck."

"Really?"

"No. I just made that up," she replies, laughing.

I shake my head. "So tell me more about you."

She shrugs, playing with a sugar packet on the table. "What do you want to know?"

"Anything. Everything."

"Not much to tell. I've lived here my whole life and never left."

"Do you have a big family?"

She shakes her head. "Just me and Mom."

I notice she bites her lip afterward, as if needing to silence herself. She doesn't go on and say anything else about her mom or her family. I sense it's a tense topic, and from what Dr. Conlan said about a rough hand, I take it maybe Marley's family situation isn't the best. I decide not to bring the mood down, and apparently, she does the same, turning the conversation to me.

"How about you? Family of doctors?"

"Yep. Dad was a doctor. Surgeon, actually. Mom's an OBGYN. I've also got a brother, Greg, but he's abandoned the family trade. He's in the army."

"Did your dad give up the surgeon gig?" she asks hesitantly.

I play with a straw paper on the table. "Sort of. He was in a terrible accident a few years back. Lost feeling in his right hand, so his surgery days are over. He still does some instructing and mentoring at the hospital, but it hasn't been the same."

"I'm sorry to hear that."

"Yeah, it's been tough. But he's been so happy I'm following in his footsteps. I guess he feels like he can live vicariously and all that."

"They must be proud of you." She seems to weigh my expression, studying me carefully.

"Yeah. This is what Dad always wanted for me."

"So, are you planning on moving back to California once you're done here?"

"That's the plan. Mom and Dad own a lot of land and set aside some for me. I'm planning to build a house once I'm done here, and get a job at the hospital my dad worked in. Dad's already practically got my name up on the wall there. He wanted to get me into the program there, but it didn't work out. Residency can be competitive. I put down Rosewood on a whim because a friend of mine did. Didn't think I'd end up here, but it's not so bad. Dad is already working on getting me into the hospital back home. It's just a given I'll go back."

She studies me as if she wants to prod me further.

53

She opens her mouth to ask something but stops. She's probably worried it's too awkward for a first... well, whatever this is.

She clarifies, "All set in stone, huh? You know where you're going."

"Is that a bad thing?" I ask, not sure what she's thinking. Not sure how to read a girl like her.

"I don't think so. Hell, I'm the opposite and look where that got me." She readjusts her hat before turning and glancing out the hazy windows at the sidewalk.

"You seem like you have it together. You have to do what's right for you."

She turns back to me, her gaze fixed on me. "Yeah, I guess. But if you don't have a plan, it makes it a little tougher to figure that all out."

"So, what do you really want to do?" I ask, really wanting to know.

She shrugs. "Get out of here. Travel. See somewhere else. Do something to inspire my writing. I love writing, but I feel like I haven't even seen the world. How can I really capture life?"

"Seems like you've seen a lot of life right here."

"I've tried to make the best of it. But it feels like I'm standing still sometimes, like I haven't really seen anything, you know?"

"So why don't you get out of here? Go travel. Live the life you want," I urge, meaning it, studying this girl who has wild eyes.

"I don't know. It's not so simple, I guess." She fidgets

54

with a packet of sugar now, as if this is dredging up some rough thoughts. I stare at her, trying to figure out the girl across from me, but a piece of me knows it won't be that simple.

"I think it's as simple as doing what you want. Life is simple if you follow what your heart wants." It's something my mom's always said. It seems like the right thing to say, but once it's out, it feels completely wrong.

Marley tears the corner of the sugar packet, some granules falling to the table. She sweeps them around, swirling them in patterns mindlessly before she looks up at me, a weak smile on her face. "Life's never simple, Alex. I might not have lived much of life yet, but I've lived enough to know that."

Looking at her, I see some pain written on her face. It's subtle, but it's there. Something about Marley isn't quite whole. Something's left her a little broken. I don't know what it is.

In truth, I don't know a lot about being broken. My life hasn't been perfect—but damn close. Good childhood memories filled with apple pie, board game nights, parents in the sporting event stands cheering for me, and birthday parties every year. A supportive yet stern set of parents who expected me home by curfew and demanded perfect grades. A family who could afford to send me to college, and who encouraged me to do so. Parents who supported my med school dreams, leaving me with few loans compared to my colleagues. In truth,

I've had it pretty easy.

Not that I haven't worked. I have. I've said no to plenty of nights out, to plenty of dates, to plenty of get-wasted kind of scenarios. I've spent years with my head in the books, my only company a cup of coffee. I've spent years in the library. I've been lonely.

But overall, I've been blessed.

Sitting here, the smell of greasy cheesesteaks permeating the room, I get the feeling Marley and I come from very different worlds and have very different experiences.

When our cheesesteaks finally come, though, and I take a bite, we simultaneously say, "Delicious" through a mouthful of cheesy goodness.

Smiling, I nod as I swallow a huge bite. "Best damn cheesesteak around. You were right."

"That's right, California boy. We might be small, but we have something to offer."

"Yes, yes you do," I agree, a greasy sandwich in the middle of nowhere making me forget about everything for a moment.

***

Simple.

That's what our first day together is. It's nothing fancy, nothing like back in California. There aren't any exorbitant dinners or suit-and-tie affairs. There are no wild nightclubs or crazy nightlife. It's a hike, a cheesesteak, and a walk through town, the girl in the red hat walking beside me, talking animatedly about childhood memories and "hot spots" in town we'll just have to see eventually.

It's the quietest, simplest date—if we're calling it that—I've ever been on.

And it's the best damn one, too.

We amble down Main Street after I offer to walk Marley home, deciding I better catch some sleep before my early shift tomorrow. We walk slowly, though, as if neither one of us is ready to quite let go of the magic from today, of the togetherness. I'm a little nervous that maybe this is just a one-time thing, a one-time tour, despite our talk about skating rinks and other places we'll see together. I don't want to take the risk that I won't see her again. In truth, I don't want to let the black-haired, zany girl go.

Marley's talking animatedly about fishing and the adorable summer festival that comes in June. She's a hand talker, her delicate hands waving around as she speaks, her whole face lighting up with discussions of funnel cakes, lemonade, and karaoke contests. I find myself smiling a cheesy grin just walking beside her, just listening to her.

She's contagious.

As we round the bend, me hanging back just a step or two to let her lead the way, my heart stops at a horrifying sight.

This is it. The perfect day, the perfect moment is over.

Chapter Five

Alex

I jump in front of Marley, instinct taking over again, shoving her behind me, my arms wrapped around her.

Despite my pounding heart, I put myself in front of her, protecting her again as the biggest dog I've ever seen comes barreling at us.

This is how I die, a beautiful girl behind me. This is where it all ends, I think, as I wince and shudder in anticipation of the pain that will soon be mine.

***

Eyes squeezed shut, I wait for the teeth to sink into my arms or legs. I'd be lying if I said I wasn't terrified, but more than fear, I'm worried. I need to protect Marley. I need to make sure she's safe.

But instead of the ear-splitting scream I expect to hear or the feeling of the horse-sized dog's jaws locked on me, something very different happens.

Marley laughs in my ear, and I feel a huge body against me, a tail flapping against my knee cap so hard I stumble a bit.

When I open my eyes to assess the situation, I see the huge, brindle dog's tail is in fact wagging, whapping me over and over as he nuzzles up to Marley. There's slobber on my shirt, but no sign of a bite.

"Henry, looks like you scared my friend here," Marley says as I finally let her out of my arms. She looks at me, shaking her head, still laughing. I can't tell if she's laughing at me or the fact that the dog is slurping her face with his ginormous tongue as she stoops down to his level.

I take a step back as the dog turns to me, coming at me. My heart jolts a little again and I put my arms out.

"Alex, he's harmless. Really. He's a good boy, aren't you, Henry?" Marley coos, rubbing his ears.

The mastiff that caused my life to flash before my eyes is now nudging me with his nose, whining a little for me to presumably pet him. I hold back.

Marley eyes me suspiciously. "Please don't tell me you're not a dog person," she demands.

I try to hide the fear and disgust on my face as the dog inches closer. "It's nothing personal. I'm sure Henry's great. But I'm just…."

Marley stands, arms crossed. "Don't tell me Mr. Hotshot Doctor is afraid of dogs?"

I put my hands in my pocket, shaking her off. "No, I'm not afraid. It's just…."

Marley raises an eyebrow. "You're afraid. Hence the death grip on my arms when Henry came out of his yard."

"Well, he's a strange dog. I didn't know."

Marley smiles. "He's hardly strange. He's lived here for seven years, since Mrs. Fritz saved him from the pound. Haven't you, Henry? Good boy. He knows I carry treats for him," she offers, pulling a biscuit out of the pocket in her dress. The biscuit is so small, it's like the dog is eating a crumb.

"I do think it's cute, though," Marley adds to me as she continues patting the dog.

"What?"

"The fact you were willing to throw yourself in front of a two-hundred-pound dog for me."

"Well, listen, I didn't dive off the bridge just for you to die in a dog mauling incident."

Marley smiles. "Okay. So, you're not afraid of dogs and you just were being selfish when you saved me. I get it."

I stutter and stammer, trying to come up with a response, but I'm tongue-tied.

I take a step forward instead, boldly giving Henry a single pat on the head. There. I'll show her she's wrong.

But then Henry turns his head, probably thinking I have a treat. The heart-stopping thing happens again. The flashbacks to the five-year-old me being attacked by a Great Dane happens again. I yank my hand back and let out an embarrassing scream that sounds more like the five-year-old me than the man version.

Marley giggles. "I'm sorry. I just... you're an ER doctor, for God's sake. You must see all kinds of horrific things."

"I do. Including dog bites."

"He won't hurt you. Trust me."

"And that's what my neighbor said about Boris, the Great Dane that attacked me as a boy and sent me to the hospital."

Marley's face straightens. "Oh my God, sorry. I didn't know. Makes sense then, I guess."

"You guess? You think a shredded leg at five explains it?" I tease, nudging her with my elbow.

"Well, I still can't imagine not liking dogs. I'd have ten if I could."

"Crazy dog lady instead of crazy cat lady, then?"

"All the way," she beams, still petting Henry. "Okay, buddy, time to go home." She points toward the white-picket-fenced yard, and Henry nuzzles against her one more time before heading presumably home.

I feel the tension in my body give way a little bit.

"So at least I know the truth about the dog thing, now," Marley says, flashing me a look and a smile as we continue on our way.

Hands in my pockets, I stare at her, trying to read her face. "And?"

"And," she begins, "I'm just wondering if your motives for saving my life from the wicked beast

Henry were truly about not wanting to waste your first rescue attempt."

"I mean, it is my solemn duty to protect life, right?"

"Yeah, I suppose, Doctor." The way she stares at me, though, says quite a lot.

It says that despite her love for dogs, she might be okay with a man who is a little bit afraid of them, even if it's ridiculous.

It also says maybe I'm not the only one feeling whatever this is between us.

"Well, all I have to say is, if you stick around long enough, maybe Henry can change your mind a little bit. About dogs and everything."

"Oh, I think this town might change a lot," I respond, then worry it's too much too fast.

When we get to Marley's house, I wonder if she's going to invite me in.

But at the corner of her lot, she stops, appraising the driveway.

"Mom's home, I guess," she rasps.

I self-consciously run a hand through my hair, wondering again if she's going to invite me in, wondering if I'm going to meet her mom.

But it must be too much too fast, because she doesn't.

"Hope you had a good time seeing this place," she says.

"I did. I'll see you for coffee, maybe tomorrow?" I ask, trying not to be too presumptuous.

"You betcha," she responds. From anyone else, it would sound annoying, but from Marley, her smoky voice makes it sound more like a tantalizing invitation than a weird phrase.

And before I can doubt her or what today meant to her, she leans in, gives me a quick kiss on the cheek, and turns to head down her sidewalk.

I like that with Marley, there's no guessing, not really. Because it seems like with Marley, you get exactly what you see.

And right now, her swift, graceful body heading through the door, I like what I see a hell of a lot.

Chapter Six

Marley

"Something hot and steamy just came through the door, and it's not a latte," Becca whispers in my ear too loudly.

Either Becca's chipper attitude is rubbing off on me, or Alex is getting to me more than I'd like to admit, because I know exactly who just walked through the door before I even turn around—and I'm smiling hugely because of it.

Like goofy grin huge.

I tell myself to act natural before pouring the next drink.

"Can I help you?" Becca asks.

"Yeah, I'm just here for a coffee," the voice says. I involuntarily shiver from the sound of it. I try to cover it by quickly delivering Mr. Joseph's latte.

"Oh, hey," I say, pretending I didn't know he was there, pretending I didn't just practically have a coronary at the thought of the sexy doctor I spent the day frolicking with being here.

"Hey, Marley. How are you?" he asks.

I remind myself again to play it cool. I remind myself we were only on a semidate yesterday, that it might not mean anything at all. I tell myself he's some California doctor, and I'm just a small-town barista. We have so little in common, and I probably just imagined all those looks, all those sparks yesterday.

But when he looks at me, those perfectly blue eyes piercing me to the core, I know I'm not imagining it.

I know he's not just here for the coffee.

This black-haired, Converse sneakers girl has snagged the sexy, supersmart doctor. I don't know how the hell it happened, but I think he's under my super odd, not-so-charming spell.

And I don't know how the hell it happened, but I think I kind of like charming him.

I feel an elbow in my ribs as Becca nudges me. Shit. I've been stupidly staring at him like a lovestruck teenager for way too long to be natural.

There it goes. I have no flirting capabilities, and I have no ability to act smoothly.

I snap out of my dead stare and head for the coffee machine, grabbing the wrong size of coffee cup.

"He ordered a large," Becca says, the cheerleader whine tainting her usually chipper voice.

"Oh, right."

"It's fine. No big deal," he comments.

"Oh, Jesus. Will you two get a room? I can feel you making love with your freaking eyes, and it's just wrong," Dane quips, bursting across the shop. "It's making us all ill."

I feel myself blush, and Becca grins. Neither Alex nor I move.

"Here's your coffee," I blurt awkwardly, as if nothing's just happened. I stand for a long moment, wondering if he's going to run for the door, head to work, and leave me wondering if I'm truly imagining everything.

"So," he says, also seeming a little awkward. "Yesterday was awesome, but we didn't get to really see any sit-down restaurants. Do you have a favorite?"

I shrug. "Lou Lou's Diner is my favorite. Not super fancy, but super delicious."

Alex nods. "This town is pretty big and everything. I don't want to get lost, and I have no idea what to order. Want to play tour guide again? Want to come with me at, say, eight? I know it will be a little late, but I work until then."

I smile. "Really? This is a big town? I hope you're kidding. And, anyway, won't you be too tired?"

Alex shrugs. "I mean, I could rustle up some energy to go eat some food, if you can. My treat, of course."

"Of course. Tour guides do get paid, after all, right?"

"Right. And this is strictly professional and all, right?" He gives me a wink meant to be creepy. And it is creepy. But it makes me shiver a little, too.

66

"Right."

"Oh, Jesus. Remind me to call poor Lou Lou and let her know some PDA is coming her way," Becca murmurs, and I laugh a little.

"Well, maybe after you show him the diner, you could show him the only hotel in town, too," Dane says.

I shake my head, pretending to be offended... but clearly not.

Dammit, Marley. Settle it down. Don't act like you haven't had sex in fifteen and a half months—not that I'm counting, obviously.

"Anyway," I continue, trying to shift the conversation as Alex pretends to warm his hands on his coffee cup. "Eight is perfect. Come get me at my house?"

"You betcha," he answers, prompting me to crinkle my nose.

"That's my line, doctor boy."

And with a smile, he's out the door. I notice he slows down as he walks by the window, taking another quick peek at me.

Even after he's gone, my smile isn't.

Dammit, I'm falling. Falling head over heels hard, spilling coffee all morning, mind making mental pictures of us kissing, of our first time, of the hotel.

"You're a goner this time, Marley," Becca says. "It's written all over your face. When you fell from that bridge, I think you fell for him, too."

"Is it obvious?"

"Uh-huh," Dane agrees, leaning on the counter.

I exhale loudly, a mixture of anticipation for what's coming mixed with fear.

Because I've learned a little bit about life during my small-town stint.

And one thing is love never, ever works out, at least not for this girl.

***

By 7:45 p.m., I've changed my outfit twice. I've traded my dark lipstick for a lighter, brighter pink, and I've brushed my hair more times in one night than I usually do all week. I'm usually pretty low-maintenance because, well, when you live in a town with about five eligible bachelors, all of whom you've already slept with at one point and decided against, looking like a cover girl isn't exactly a priority.

But Alex has me all messed up. Suddenly, mascara and lipstick are a priority. It's like I've been reawakened, like my hope and heart have been thawed. It's like being pulled out of the chilling water dislodged something inside I'd thought was gone.

Don't get ahead of yourself. You don't know him that well yet.

And it's true. My head is holding me back. Those sparks between us feel so nice, so inviting. But the truth is this guy could turn out to be a serial killer—although it seems unlikely since he did save my life. He could have a ton of baggage, or he could decide my baggage is too much. To him, this late summer romance could be a fling of desperation. Those looks, that lust I see in his eyes could just be his manhood talking and not his heart. This is all happening too fast.

I'm not usually this easy, really. I'm difficult and reserved when it comes to love. I've been burned so many times my heart is warped. Still, something about those eyes, about his voice, lures me in. I've only spent a few hours with him, but it's like this indescribable force within wants me to know more. Something tells me he could be just what I've been looking for. The dependable to my instability, the calm to my crazy. He could be the rational to my let's get lost mentality, and the reality to my dreamer-like state. He could be the hand beside me, the encouragement to do more. He's the one who will rein me in when I get too out of control but let me be free when it's time to fly after those dreams.

He seems like just what my life is missing.

But just because I want it to be true, just because I've painted the scene in my head of us together, doesn't mean it'll work. He's from California, a goal-oriented realist who got stuck in this place. I'm just a small-town nobody going nowhere slowly. I'm a rebel without a cause, a mess, and a dreamer without any wings at all.

We're unlikely to work out, and whatever this is will most likely crash and burn. My scarred heart will get another battle wound, and I'll be left behind the coffee machine with burning eyes and a bitter taste in my mouth.

When the knock at the door heralds me forward, though, my heart flutters with the possibility. Tossing open the door, I see him, my unlikely knight who saved me already, flowers in his hand.

They're daisies. My favorite.

Can this guy get any more perfect? And what is he doing with me?

"Ready to go?" he asks, peeking in.

I nod, feeling a little self-conscious about our lackluster home. I spent a few hours cleaning up this afternoon for this reason.

"Yeah, let's go."

"Is your mom home?" he inquires, eyeing me and looking around. I think he wants me to invite him in.

"No. She's actually at work." And by actually, I mean she finally went.

Alex just nods. "Okay, let's go."

And just like that, we're off to dinner at Lou Lou's. The talk is easy and fast. We converse about work and the news. We carry on like we've been doing this for years. We're different in so many ways, yet the conversation flows. Even when the talking ceases, there are no weird pauses or cringe-worthy moments, other than my tripping over the uneven sidewalk.

There's just us, a guy and a girl heading for a late dinner in the town where I grew up, where I never imagined to be going out with such an amazing guy.

At Lou Lou's, Alex lets me order for him. I get us my favorite—the pierogi special and an order of nachos. As we share and laugh over our food, I feel myself relax into it all.

In the middle of dinner, Alex's cell phone rings. He checks the screen. "It's my mom. I'll call her later," he says.

"Don't be ridiculous," I respond. "Go ahead."

"You sure?"

"Positive. I'll get to eat more of the nachos while you're talking," I joke, shoving one in my mouth for dramatic effect.

He nods, clicking the button on his phone. "Hey, Mom. What's up?"

I feel a little odd suddenly, as if I'm listening in on an intimate conversation. Alex doesn't look alarmed though.

"Yeah, maybe over Thanksgiving? That would be great. I miss you. I know... how's Greg? ... Great. Uh-huh."

I smile, watching Alex talk to his mom, sensing the connection just from the look on his face. I can't imagine what it must be like to be so close, even though they're physically so far apart.

"I love you, Mom. I have to go. I'm out with someone," he says. "Of course... yes... uh-huh. Love you too, Mom. Bye."

Alex clicks the phone, rolling his eyes. "Sorry. She's just concerned about me being so far away.

You'd think I was sixteen or something."

I grin. "It's fine. No worries. She's just being a mom."

"You don't think I'm a mama's boy, right?" he asks, grinning, but I'm not sure he's teasing.

"For the record, no. And for the record, I don't think being a mama's boy is bad. Having a mom that loves you like she clearly loves you is a good thing. Your family sounds awesome."

It's true. I'd give anything to have a mom in my corner the way Alex clearly does. I'd give anything to have an over-the-top somewhat meddling mother.

Because I've seen the alternative.

Not that I blame my mom. She's made her mistakes, sure, but she's also been dealt some tough cards. It's not her fault, I remind myself. Even when I want to blame her, I can't. It's not all her fault. She loves me the best she can.

We continue dinner, talking more about Alex's family and childhood. I strategically leave most of mine out, only focusing on the good stuff. I'm not ready to cross that bridge yet—no inside joke intended—even if we are out on a date.

When we leave the diner though, I'm feeling more confident. I'm feeling like we've taken a huge jump. I'm feeling like this thing with Alex isn't just a tour guide kind of thing.

This might not work out. We might not be made for each other. This might all be temporary.

But for right now, whatever this is, whatever label we put on it, I'm happy. The girl on the bridge that night seems like a distant memory.

"So, tour guide, what is our next attraction going to be?" Alex asks as he walks me home.

"Tour guide, huh? So, do you take all your tour guides on dates?" I ask coyly.

"Only the ones who wear supercute red hats," he says.

"And how many of those are there?"

"One. There's only one."

When we get to my house, this time he leans in to kiss me on the cheek. I think about turning, catching his lips within mine, the mere thought of it sending a jolt to all kinds of places.

But I don't. I don't want to rush this. I want to savor it, take it all in, and drink in this crazy thing growing between us.

Because I'm not standing still anymore. With Alex, I feel breathless, like I'm running a marathon without a finish line.

And I hope to hell the finish line doesn't come into view anytime soon.

Chapter Seven

Marley

I wake up the next morning when the sun streams into my room, even the weather seeming to mimic my sunny mood. For once, the prospect of waking up doesn't seem like such a bad thing. Life doesn't seem so gray.

I feel like one of those cheesy girls in the movies, but I can't help it.

I've got the day off, but Alex is working all day. We exchanged phone numbers last night, and although I try to tell myself I'm just checking for emergency messages, my heart skips a beat when I see a text.

Alex: I had a great time last night. I'll call you after work to make plans for our next adventure.

I exhale with a smile, stretching my arms toward the sky.

I don't want to get ahead of myself. I don't want to get my hopes up. But I think it's too late for that.

Suddenly, life doesn't feel like this monotonous game of waiting for something to happen. Alex's happened.

With a day of emptiness—the good kind, this time—ahead of me, I toss on my favorite outfit, add my red hat, and grab my journal, heading to the kitchen to grab a to-go cup of coffee to take to my favorite spot.

When I get to the kitchen, though, I startle.

She's here. She's up already. Seeing Mom up and dressed now—really at any time—is a miracle.

"Hey," I utter, my mood turning serious automatically.

"Marley," Mom says neutrally. She's sitting at the table, a wrinkled gray T-shirt on. Her hair's standing up in every direction.

"How was work last night?" I ask.

She shrugs. "I only stayed for half my shift. Didn't feel well."

I bite my lip, swallowing the building anger. "Where'd you go then?"

She glares at me. "None of your business, Marley. I'm not a fucking child."

I inhale, reminding myself to build the patience I don't have much of anymore.

"Mom, I'm just worried about you. Charlotte called me last week and said you've been missing a lot of your shifts. I'm just…. I don't want you slipping again."

I feel tears stinging in my eyes, the familiar tears of past pain. I feel the tears from my teenage years—

tears over Dad's death, then the tears of fear of losing another parent. I feel the searing agony of when I went to live with Margaret and Joe for a few months when Mom was away. I feel all the hurt well up from the past few years, the constant worry about her slipping again and the hellish guilt when she did over and over again.

"Marley, I'm fine. I'm not perfect, but no one is. I'm fine. I'm doing my best."

Mom's face, grayer than usual today, is marked by hardship. The fine lines age her well beyond her actual age. Most of all, though, the pain in her eyes screams at me.

If I've known pain, she's known sheer horror.

I remind myself she is, in fact, doing her best. Best for Mom is a little different than some would consider, but I've learned to love her harder for it. She needs me.

"Do you work today?" I ask gently, heading to pour myself a cup of coffee.

"No. I'm going to stay in today."

I sigh. She probably is on the schedule, but I know better than to ask.

"I'm heading to the park for a while. Do you want to come?"

She just shakes her head, heading to the sofa to tuck herself under the old plaid flannel blanket and fall asleep.

And just like that, our interaction is over. Even though Mom says she's not the child, I sigh to myself, tears still singeing my eyes.

She may not be the child, but she's also not the mom here.

When Dad's life ended, I didn't just lose one parent. I lost two.

Heading to the park, the sun still shining, the day still empty like it was when I got up, my optimism is slipping away.

Nothing's changed, yet, just like so many times in life, everything, everything has changed.

***

The words won't come.

I sit and stare at a blank page in a new journal, the one I hoped to start today. Something about Alex, about our few times together, has made me feel a new resolve to pursue my writing, to write out my heart.

But now, the stark reminder this morning that Mom's never going to be completely okay again slaps me in the face.

No matter what happens, no matter what I do, I can't leave.

I just can't leave. I'll always be standing right here.

I want to hate Dad for what he did. I want to hate how he took all our seminormal lives and crushed them with one decision. I want to curse him out, curse out the universe for taking Mom's happiness and her hope for the future. With it, it took my own.

Margaret and Joe have talked to me over and over. It's not my fault. It's not my responsibility. They'll help in any way they can.

But, how can they? They aren't her daughter. They can't possibly know her, care for her like I can.

And how can I abandon her?

My dad already did, and look how that worked out. How can I, knowing the pain she's battled every day since that fateful night, leave her alone?

She's not perfect. Hell, some would argue she's not even deserving of my love. There have been plenty of times I've come second to all sorts of things. Boyfriends and alcohol have stolen my mother over the years for stints of time. I spent plenty of nights alone and scared. I spent plenty of nights with Margaret and Joe, pretending I just wanted to visit when, in truth, I just didn't want to go home alone.

I spent years worrying I'd get that knock on the door, that phone call that she, too, was gone. I spent years worrying there'd be a knock on the door taking me away to a new life, to strangers, because someone found out Mom's secrets.

I spent those months Mom was "getting help" feeling helpless, feeling lost.

And I vowed to myself, smiling for the first time since Dad died, I'd never leave her.

She'd walked in the door, home from one of her times away to recover. I was seventeen, and it was her fourth stint—this time, for rehab for alcoholism.

"Marley, I missed you. I'm sorry, baby. I'm sorry for everything. I don't ever want to leave you again," she'd said, and my seventeen-year-old self clung to those words like a miracle. Mom was back. I wouldn't leave her. I would make sure she never went away.

Now, the promise seems like a pipe dream. I didn't leave, but I still lost her over the years. Her battles with the bottle and depression have made keeping her happy a daily struggle. Guilt racks me even now for losing the battle with her.

But to leave would be to give up completely. I can't do that.

I lean my head against the solid oak tree, feeling pity rise for Mom, for me.

For the whole situation.

"Why'd you have to do it, Dad? Why weren't we enough?" I whisper into the silent breeze, only a few buzzing bees around to hear my plea.

I swipe at the tears. I know I should hate him. I know I want to.

But I can't.

Because the pain we feel in his absence must be nothing to the agony he felt that night. I don't understand what drove him to it. I probably never will.

But I do know that night on the Cedar Bend Bridge was a night I can't even imagine. To do what he did, to leave us like that, it must have been some hell he was going through.

Thinking about it, my mind goes to a more recent place, to the night Alex found me.

Alex.

He's an amazing man. And sure, he's probably not perfect. But hell, he's a whole lot more perfect than me.

My family's baggage is too much. *I'm* too much.

I can pretend to the world I'm all okay, that Marley's this sassy, sarcastic, strong girl. But deep down, I'm broken. Every piece of me is just a jagged shard waiting to stab into everyone around me, into everything I touch. No matter how good things feel with him, I know it'll never go anywhere. It can't.

Once he finds out just how broken I am, he's going to realize even he, a doctor, can't fix me. Some things, some people just simply can't be patched.

***

When I finally trek home, I'm feeling glum. I've gotten myself into the way too common Marley funk, and I hate I'm letting all this family stuff put a damper on how happy I was this morning.

I pause at my door, knowing going home isn't what I need.

I turn around, walking one house over, to my refuge. This is exactly what I need, like so many other times in life.

I don't bother knocking, knowing Margaret will be on the back porch with Smoky.

"Hello," I yell into the Cape Cod once I swing open the familiar yellow door. I always loved that sunshine-yellow door. It screams "welcome."

"I'm out back, dear," Margaret yells. In her inviting voice, though, it sounds more like she's singing.

I traipse down the hallway and through the kitchen, swinging open the screen door to the familiar screened-in porch. My mood instantly lightens at the sight of my favorite place.

Margaret is dressed in a pink pantsuit, Smoky purring on her lap as she scratches his chin. She's got her English Breakfast tea on the mosaic stand beside her.

I notice there's a second cup on the other stand by my spot on the glider.

I smile.

"How'd you know I was coming?" I ask, sitting down beside her, grabbing the steaming cup and warming my hands, putting my face over the liquid that always instills nostalgia in me. I spent so many afternoons here as a teenager, right here, gliding on Margaret and Joe's porch, feeling love and peace, something I didn't get at home. This porch was my sanctuary, my refuge, my safe spot.

Margaret smiles, readjusting her glasses and fluffing her perfectly permed hair. "I just had a hunch, I guess. It's good to see you."

I smile. "You, too. Sorry it's been a while. Work has been keeping me busy."

Margaret winks at me. "Just work, Marley Jade? Come on. You know I have ears and eyes all over this town."

I give Margaret what I hope to be a look that discounts the rumors. Instead, a smile spreads on my face. "So I may have had a few adventures with the new doctor in residency."

"You mean the hunk who saved you, huh?"

"Margaret, we've been through this. It wasn't a big deal. I was just being klutzy."

Margaret had swung by the day after the fall with flowers and a worried expression, even though Joe had explained to her numerous times I was fine.

"I've heard the doctor in residency is spending every free moment with Rosewood's favorite black-haired girl. I think it's great, honey. I swung by the hospital myself the other day just to scope him out. Seems like a great man."

I shrug. "Yeah, he is." No sense in denying it. I raise the tea to my lips, blowing on it, my eyes traveling to the tropical plant in the corner of the porch, my favorite here.

"What's wrong?" she asks.

I turn and look back at her. She's studying me with a frown.

"Nothing."

"Don't nothing me. I know you too well, Marley Jade. You're forgetting I can always tell when something is wrong. Tell me."

I sigh. No use lying to Margaret. She's got intuition that's so strong, she knows when I'm going to be stopping by. "I'm just... worried."

"About what?"

"I think this whole thing with Alex, although fun and wonderful, might just be a waste of time. He's a doctor. From California. And I'm... me."

Margaret extends her hand toward me, patting my hand. "And you're wonderful, Marley. Don't be ridiculous. That boy is lucky to get time with you."

I smile. "I think you might be biased."

"So what if I am? You're an amazing girl. Don't give me this load of crap about him being better than you."

I shake my head. Margaret never minces words. "I'm just worried he's going to be scared away by my past. It's messy. You know that better than anyone. I have a lot of baggage. And with Mom the way she is...."

"Honey, we've been telling you for years you can't let the past or your mom hold you back from your own happiness. It's not your responsibility. I know you love her, and you're an amazing girl for sticking by her through everything. But Marley, you have to let go, even a little. You can't let everything that's happened be a roadblock."

I sigh. "You make it sound so easy, so logical."

"I didn't say it was easy. You know why? Because you have such a big heart. Your heart's so big, you feel everyone's pain. And your family has a lot of it, I know. But I want you to find happiness. I want you to be brave enough to try. And if that happiness is with Alex, then go for it. Life's never easy, and everyone has their baggage. Your hunky doctor isn't perfect either, I'm sure. He has his issues and complexities, no doubt. But that's the thing. Everyone does. If you can find someone who makes those struggles seem a little less, who makes it seem bearable, then cling to that. Don't be afraid to show him all of you, every part of you, even the hard parts. Because there are so many good pieces to you. So many. And if he's half the guy I think he is, your cracked pieces aren't going to scare him away. They're going to make him love you more."

I inhale, feeling the happiness of the morning seep back in. Margaret always grounds me. She always makes me feel better, makes me feel like I can be happy.

"I just worry. Because if I find too much happiness, I'm afraid it'll take me away from her. And I don't think she can handle it. She's not well today."

"Your mom is stronger than you think. She needs to find the bravery to be happy again too. I still haven't given up on the fact she will. But until then, you know Joe and I are here. We'll watch over her. You're both like family to us."

Now I reach over and squeeze her hand, thankful for this angel in my life.

"I love you," I say to her.

"I love you, too, Marley Jade."

I smile, taking a sip of my tea, thankful to have such an amazing woman who helped me feel the love my mom sometimes couldn't show.

And for helping me, even now, see what I need most of all.

Chapter Eight

Alex

I flip through the pages of the medical encyclopedia, it's dusty brown cover barely legible at this point. This relic from the past doesn't really have much practical use with the invention of Google. Still, as I run my hand over the cover, sitting in my bed with the blankets kicked off, I can't help but smile, thinking about the day he gave this to me.

I remember being twelve and flipping through the worn pages, mouth open in amazement at all the words I couldn't pronounce and at all the amazing things. From that moment on, I knew. My fate was sealed.

I wanted to be just like him.

I set the encyclopedia back on the nightstand by the picture of Dad. I'm about thirteen in the picture, and we're standing in front of the biggest roller coaster at Disney. My dad makes bunny ears behind me, his mustache not hiding his smile. It's one of my favorite pictures because it's one of the few vacations we took together, one of the few times he could pull himself away from the hospital long enough to just let loose and have fun.

"Life is work, if you're doing it right, Alex." That was what Dad always said to me, since the time I could talk.

Not that it's bad advice. Mom and Dad have a good life, and they gave me and Greg a good life because of their work. I see the pride in my parents' eyes when they talk about their achievements, about how many people they've helped. I see the pride when Dad cruises down the street in his BMW and when Mom pulls into the driveway of our huge, gorgeous house.

Money can't buy happiness, but hard work can buy you things you can be proud of. This is also something I've learned along the way.

I sigh, staring up at my ceiling. It's eleven o'clock, and I have to be back for the morning shift. I should be doing something productive—sleeping, studying, reading medical case studies. Something.

But here I am, staring at the ceiling, listening to the single clock tick from the kitchen. The silence of the apartment, usually a welcome accompaniment to my studies, haunts me.

It's lonely. It's dull. How the hell have I survived this long?

Suddenly, this one-bedroom apartment filled with medical books and a few necessities seems like a barren wasteland. I feel the monotony of my days kicking in. Work, eat, sleep a few hours, and study. That's it.

I don't think it would matter if it was a five-story mansion or if a Rolls Royce was parked in the driveway. The loneliness would still seep right in, maybe even more.

I don't know why it's getting to me now. This isn't something new. I've carved this life path out for years. I've gone willingly into this arena.

It's always been good enough. It's always been more than enough. I've never needed anything more than this, my eyes set on that surgeon title, my shoes following in Dad's footsteps like I promised him all those years ago.

But something's shifted, and that something started with a girl falling off a bridge and yanking me down with her into the unknown.

In our few encounters, though, I've come to realize the unknown isn't such a bad thing, and life isn't exciting because of where you live. It's who you're spending your life with. Marley can make even Rosewood seem full of adventure. From cheesesteaks to diners to hikes in the woods, I've lived more in the few moments I spent with her than probably the past ten years. I've experienced. I've breathed in a life I've been shoving away.

And now, dammit, the life I thought was going so well seems—dull. Pointless. Endless.

It's crazy because in the past few years, I tried my

best to shove all women away. I told myself matters of the heart weren't for me, not with my goal requiring so much energy. I promised myself I'd achieve my goals first and then worry about love.

Yet, here I am, alone at eleven o'clock at night thinking about a girl in a red hat whom I just met a few weeks ago. A girl who is named after Bob Marley and who loves wearing her Converse sneakers with everything. A girl with a smoky voice and a penchant for laughter, who loves writing poetry and loves rain. A girl who sucked me right in without me even noticing.

And not only that—she's made me feel like everything I thought I had before her was so empty.

I pull out my phone and smile to see a text from her.

Marley: Swing by for coffee after work tomorrow? I want to show you something else.

Me: Deal. Looking forward to it.

I toss my phone to the nightstand and reach for something I haven't since I started my residency—the remote. Instead of spending the next few hours with my nose buried in my books, I do something that feels a little wrong.

I flip on some reality television, not even a medical show mind you, and waste a few hours in someone else's life, wishing all the while tomorrow would come fast.

***

"So, where are we off to next, tour guide?" I ask,

startling Marley who is pouring a coffee. I got through my ten-hour shift and, although I'm exhausted, I'm energized by the thought of spending more time with her.

Today, she's wearing a red sundress, her Converse sneakers, and her signature hat. I'm starting to think she sleeps in it.

"Well, I thought we'd check out the park at the edge of town. I used to love it as a little girl. It's peaceful, totally Zen."

"Zen sounds good right about now," I respond as she hands me a coffee.

"Rough day?"

"Just the usual. Busy, busy. A few broken bones, a car accident, and some fevers. Nothing too traumatic. Just... I have a lot to learn."

"Don't we all," Marley says, smiling as she undoes her apron.

"Oh, hey Alex. Back again so soon?" Becca asks, leaning over the register and winking at me.

"Becca, how long until your classes start?"

"A week."

"Oh, man. We'll miss you so much," Marley jokes, smiling to soothe the sarcasm in her voice.

"Don't worry. I'll be back for winter break. You two will probably be freaking married by then."

Marley shakes her head, rolling her eyes at the perky blonde. I just nod at her to say goodbye as Marley comes out from behind the counter and heads out the door.

"Freedom," she yells into the sky, the sun beaming down on her. "Isn't it the best feeling? Getting off work, finally free to do whatever?"

I shrug. "I guess."

Marley gives me an eye. "You guess? Oh no, don't tell me you're one of those workaholics."

"I think you'd be pressed to find a doctor who isn't. It kind of goes with the job."

"Well, when I'm through with you, you won't be a workaholic. Nope."

I shake my head as she pulls my hand, yanking me down the sidewalk, animatedly chattering about some tourists who swung by Georgia's and a food inspector who stopped by and is annoying as hell. I sip my coffee, reveling in her storytelling.

"So, I'm yammering on and on. You must be exhausted. I'll stop talking," she says.

"No, don't. I like hearing your stories. It's entertaining."

She laughs. "You must be hard up if you think I'm entertaining. Oh, we're here," she crows, leading me through a gate toward a tiny park.

There's a bench, a swing set, and that's about it. It's small and serene, but in a good way.

She leads me to the bench, and I plop down. It feels good to get off my feet.

We sit for a moment, staring at the sunset, reveling in the silence.

And then Marley jumps up. "Look at that! It's a baby bunny. How adorable," she exclaims, quietly sneaking toward it.

I put together what she's doing. "Marley, you really shouldn't touch it. They can have ticks and all kinds of diseases," I warn, hating myself for sounding like I'm trying to be someone's mom.

Marley ignores me anyway, catching the bunny, picking it up with a huge, girlish grin. "Hey, buddy. You're so soft. Alex, come pet him," she says, holding the bunny toward me.

"I'm good."

"Oh my God. Don't be such a pansy. Come pet the damn rabbit I wrangled."

I shake my head. "Are you always this bossy? And insulting?"

"Are you always this boring? Come on. It's a rabbit, not a wolverine."

I put my coffee down on the bench and head over, eying the bug-eyed creature. It is damn cute. I pat it on the head, reminding myself to wash my hands later.

We stand for a long moment, Marley, me, and a wild rabbit. The sunset behind her loose waves, her eyes shimmering at the delight of her catch, I get a glimpse of her I haven't yet. I see who she must've been as a girl, this wild and free child full of life.

That zest for life is still there. It's just definitely a little less shimmery sometimes.

She eventually lets our newfound friend go. "Run

free, buddy," she encourages. The rabbit sits still.

She sighs. "Or stay put. Your choice."

I shake my head, reaching over to move a strand of hair from her face. "You're something else, Marley Jade. I had no idea when I came to this town I would find such a wild woman."

"Yeah, Rosewood can't quite contain me. It doesn't really know what to do with me."

"I don't think anyone does," I say, staring at her. Her pink lips practically scream at me to take them with mine. Her cheekbones, her eyes, the perfect curves of her body, they all beg me to touch them, to claim them, to ravage them.

I think she senses the longing I have because she parts her lips a little bit. I think about leaning in, about succumbing to this instinctual feeling. I want to explore Marley, to figure out what this is between us. I want to lean her back on the bench and find our own sense of freedom.

But I don't. As usual, the rational Alex takes over, the realistic, straitlaced surgeon Alex who doesn't do crazy.

What good would kissing her do? She's this wild and free woman, and I'm this boring, square guy. We're two different pieces to two different puzzles. We're from two different worlds going in two different directions.

All that will happen is heartbreak, chaos, and a loss of focus on both our parts.

So I awkwardly scratch an itch on my neck before gesturing back toward the bench.

"It's beautiful here," I say, motioning toward the park when we sit back down.

"Yeah. I could sit here all day," she agrees. "I wonder if I could just quit my job and live here in the park."

"Sounds like a pretty decent idea to me. I mean, I love my job, don't get me wrong. But sometimes I wish I didn't have somewhere I had to be all the time. Maybe the bunny doesn't have such a bad gig, huh?" We glance over at the bug-eyed rabbit, who is still sitting where Marley left him.

"Other than crazy women picking him up, I guess not."

"Man, seriously though. I have to be back at work at five." I take a sip of my coffee, trying to relish in this moment.

"Don't go," Marley says, shrugging. "You look tired. Take a break. Call off. Dr. Conlan is a forgiving man."

"I can't just call off. I'm in residency. I have to make a good impression."

"By working yourself to death? By being a bore? Come on, Alex. This is the time to live it up a bit. Explore. Have fun." She nudges me with her elbow.

I shake my head. "Have you always been like this?"

"Like what?"

"Free?"

She raises an eyebrow. "I wouldn't call it free. I've

had my demons, and I've had my moments. But, I guess in a way, the answer is yes. I made sure I lived a little. I played hooky now and then. Still do, which isn't easy in a town this small. You can't quite play sick when half the town sees you if you leave your house."

"Yeah, I bet it isn't easy."

She eyes me with a smile. "I mean, I might be stereotyping here, but I'm going to venture a guess the words 'playing hooky' aren't in your vocabulary. Let me guess. You were the kid who sat in the front row in every class, who turned his work in early, and who had perfect attendance?"

"What are you saying, I'm a boring nerd?" I scowl at her, but she just grins back.

"Am I wrong?"

"Completely," I say, nudging her with my elbow this time.

"Really?"

"Yep. I sat in the second row in every class. And I missed four days of school when I had my wisdom teeth out."

She laughs. "Oh my God. We need to get you out a little. Get you to live a little. Hell, I'm just a barista in a shitty town, but at least I can say I've had *some* fun."

"Wow. Make a guy feel like shit."

"I'm sorry. I'm not trying to. I think you're amazing and I think being a doctor is so admirable. I could obviously never do it. But come on. You also need to find balance. I've seen Dr. Conlan spend his entire life working. Like his entire life. And he's not even the worst of them. I just think you need to find a way to balance it all, you know?"

I nod. "Actually, I do. I love being a doctor, I do. But my dad was a surgeon. I've seen him work away his life too. And so many times as a kid, I asked myself why. Why wasn't he there more? Why couldn't he set the work aside? I wanted to be him, but a part of me hoped I wouldn't completely be like him. Here I am, though, following in his footsteps, and I know I'm headed for that life."

"What made you want to be a surgeon?"

"Well, like I said, that's what my dad did. I just always loved medicine, and I thought it was cool how much my dad did for people. Guess I just have been focused on living up to his expectations."

"I see. So is this what you really want then, putting your dad's thoughts aside?"

I raise an eyebrow, feeling my defenses rise. "Of course. I wouldn't do all this work if it wasn't."

"Just checking," she says before leaning against my shoulder. "Just checking."

We sit for a long time until the sun goes down, Marley leaning against my arm as if we've sat here dozens of times. Her breathing lulling me into a state of peace, I think about how much I would like to sit here for days, her leaning on my arm, the world seeming all right.

Most of all, I think about her question, wondering

if the answer I gave so quickly is really the answer I'm feeling.

Chapter Nine

Alex

My phone's incessant buzzing whips me out of dreamland, and I groggily reach for it.

The number on the screen is familiar, but one I haven't seen flash on my phone for a while.

"Hey, Dad," I practically groan, sleepiness still evident on my voice.

"Alex, how are you?" His voice is calm and stoic, the voice of reason and logic.

It's been a while since I've heard from him, but then again, we're both working insane schedules. Dad might not be a surgeon anymore, but he keeps himself active in the medical community. There isn't a week that goes by that he isn't mentoring, teaching, or attending a conference. I think his injury has only motivated him to work even more.

"I'm okay, Dad. Tired."

"How are things going? Are you doing a good job?"

"I'm trying."

He scoffs. "Trying? What the hell does that mean?"

I shake my head. "I'm trying to do a good job. It's hard. I'm exhausted."

"Well, yes, of course you are. People don't die or get hurt on the clock. Life in the ER is all about bad timing."

I stare at the ceiling, counting the tiles as I listen to Dad rationalize everything. That's Dad for you, though. Logical to a fault. Emotion doesn't have a place in his world. Maybe that's why he's been such an amazing surgeon.

It's not that my dad's an asshole or apathetic. He's got a heart—at least I think. He's just always been a man of stoicism, a man of serious realism. He's the man who doesn't believe in fluffy words.

"So how are you?"

"Well, I'm okay. But I'm worried. Your mom said you were out the other day."

I roll my eyes. Only my parents could try to keep a leash on me at this age from across the country. "Yeah, just seeing the town," I answer, a biting tone in my voice. I drag myself out of bed, plodding out of my bedroom and to the kitchen. I lean on the counter, trying to shake off the exhaustion.

"Be careful, Alex. This is the time to stay focused. Keep the hospital and your goals in sight. Don't get distracted."

"It was dinner, Dad. Relax," I say, feeling an edge

creeping in. Usually Dad's advice—or commands—don't really get to me. I know he means well. Who am I to argue with a man who's been super successful?

"I know. But I'm just saying."

"What are you saying, Dad?" I try not to exhale in annoyance like the teenager I once was. I try to remind myself to be an adult, that he's just looking out for me. I stretch as I wait for the biting advice to dart out of his mouth.

"I'm just saying this is the time to set yourself up for success. I talked to Dr. Zeigle. Do a good job these next few years and you'll have a position waiting for you. He'll take you under his wing, with me too of course, and take you through the surgical training you'll need. It's all set. You just need to do well now."

"Sounds good." Even I can detect the detachment in my own voice. News that should excite me just sounds… dry. Dull. Maybe it's the sleep I'm still trying to shake off, or maybe it's Dad's forceful nature.

"Do you realize the opportunity you've had, son? Not everyone is handed this chance."

"And Dad, maybe not everyone wants it." I move myself to the tan sofa in the living room area, plopping myself down, bracing myself for the wrath that's sure to come.

"Are you kidding me? After all your work and effort? After all the money we've invested in you, and the encouragement, you're going to toss it away now? For what, Alex? For some girl you barely know?"

"Who said anything about a girl?"

"You don't have to. There's only one thing that'll pull a man right off the path to success."

"That's ridiculous." I shake my head, fixing my gaze on the small window in the corner of the room, glancing out at the raindrops pattering against it in a wild pattern, thinking about Marley and our first hike together.

"I hope so. Because I hope you're not going to let yourself get distracted in some small-ass town. You've worked too hard. Don't let us down now."

"Okay, Dad. I won't." My answer is half-hearted. Dad's been pissed since I applied for residency here after our top choices—his top choices, that is—didn't work out. He'd blamed me, said I should've worked harder. He was pissed I came here, but decided I could make the best of it and still get things back on track. Now, though, he's probably doubting that.

"Talk to you later," he grumbles, and with that, the phone conversation is over.

I sigh, slamming the phone down on the stand near me.

It's nothing new. Dad's always been a tough-love, stern kind of guy. No I love yous, no affection. Just work and gather achievements. That's how you got Dad's stamp of approval.

Today, though, his words don't sound like the words of a man I admire. They don't sound like words that inspire me to work hard.

They sound asinine. Cold. Empty.

I squeeze the bridge of my nose between my thumb and forefinger, wondering how things got so complicated. Wondering how the hell I ended up in the middle of whatever this is.

Wondering how I got so lost.

Then again, Marley's made me wonder if maybe I was lost before I got here. Maybe the path I so carefully set out—or the path my parents set out for me—wasn't the path I wanted to follow at all.

Still, Dad's words, although aggravating, have some truth to them. I've invested years, tons of money, and so much of my effort into this. It would be pointless to give it up now. It seems wasteful to not give it my all. I've sacrificed for years for this. Can I really throw in the towel when the finish line is so close?

Can I afford to be distracted by Marley, even if it feels right?

Chapter Ten

Marley

This must be what it felt like to be Bonnie. You know, from Bonnie and Clyde.

The anxiety, the butterflies, the sweaty palms. The feeling of doing something a little crazy.

Or a lot crazy.

Okay, I'm being melodramatic. Bonnie was out robbing banks and pulling off heists. I'm simply stealing a doctor and forcing him to play hooky. Could we technically call that kidnapping?

I lean against the wall outside the entrance to the ER, trying not to look like a creepy bomber or like I'm in need of help. I try to act natural—not an easy task.

My heart flutters when I see Alex rushing toward the door, the sun beating down on us.

"Stop," I yell, stretching a hand in front of him. He startles, having to do a double take, clearly in the work zone and not the crazy girl zone.

"Marley? What's wrong?"

I smile. "You're working too much," I say, as I grab hold of his shoulders when he gets close enough, spinning him around.

"Marley, I work today. I'm supposed to be clocking in right now," he points out, looking confused as hell.

"Not today you're not."

"I can't just...." He pauses, trying to stop me from leading him away.

"Oh yes you can. It's official. Alex Evans, you're playing hooky today."

I walk in front of him, grabbing his hand and leading him toward my pickup truck in the parking lot. Everything we need for my planned kidnapping is there.

I meet with resistance when I try to yank him forward.

"Marley," he says, pulling me toward him. I spin to face him. "It sounds like fun. But I can't just up and walk out on work. I'm in residency. I can't afford to not show up."

"Well, doctor boy, lucky for you I have an in." I wriggle my eyebrow at him in what I'm sure is a creepy move. He scrunches up his face in confusion.

"You talked to Dr. Conlan?"

"Of course. Listen, I want you to be wild and free and all that. But I also don't want you losing your residency. So I cleared our hooky day with Dr. Conlan last night."

"Well, then it's not really playing hooky, is it?" Alex asks, his face finally relaxing.

"Listen, baby steps with you. Besides. The hooky part isn't the wild and free part. It's what we're doing with our hooky day."

I smile at him coyly, yanking him toward the parking lot. The tension in his body eases, and now he practically runs after me. I give myself an internal pat on the back for being so smart and coming up with this idea. The man needed to get away—again. Okay, so maybe I'm a bad influence on work ethic after all.

"What are we doing?"

"Come on. You think I'm just going to give it up like that? Not happening. And no looking in the back of my truck."

"Where's your truck?" Alex asks.

I pretend to zip my lips, not wanting to give it away.

He eyes me, then the parking lot, and takes off sprinting toward, to my chagrin, my vehicle.

"Hey, no fair! Stop right now, Alex Evans!" I shriek, running after him, holding my hat on my head with one hand.

I catch up to him, my long legs and my desire not to ruin the surprise carrying me fast. When I reach him, I slam up against his body, shoving him against the passenger door, not letting him get to the back of the truck.

Standing in the beaming sun, the black pavement of Rosewood Hospital's parking lot radiating heat beneath my flip-flops, I realize I'm standing way too close to Alex, arms pinning him back. His cologne wafts up toward me, and his firm biceps beneath my fingernails make me involuntarily shudder. I'm close enough to see every detail of his face, the crystal blue of his eyes. My heart pounds in my chest, not just from the impromptu sprint across the parking lot, but from the feeling in my gut.

"No peeking," I gasp breathily, looking up into his face, admiring every line.

"Tell me where we're going," he demands, not even fighting me.

"Not a chance. Get in and you'll find out."

He shakes his head, and I finally step back, letting him open the door. I walk around the truck to the driver side, never taking my eyes off him, giving him a warning point to keep him in line. When I get in and buckle my seat belt, I turn to Alex before starting the truck. Alex settles in, flicking the fuzzy dice hanging from the rearview mirror.

"Those happen to be my lucky dice," I say.

"Really?"

"No. But it sounds good," I admit as I start the truck. I pull out of Rosewood Hospital and head toward our destination.

"I can't believe you kidnapped me from work," Alex remarks as we head through town.

"It wasn't very hard, you know. It's not like I had to take you at knifepoint."

"Well, what kind of moron would turn down a day with a wild and fun tour guide like you?"

"The workaholic kind," I reply, grinning.

"Hey, look, I'm trying to break away."

"And I'm trying to help."

"And you won't quit until you've succeeded?" he asks, grinning.

I just glance over at him. "You betcha," I say, before cranking the music up again.

***

"Isn't it just beautiful?" I ask after stabilizing myself, rowing carefully out past Alex. There's a gentle breeze that lifts the ends of my hair. It's a warm day, but the perfect kind of warm, not stifling.

Alex sails over the water behind me, looking perfectly at home in his kayak as we ease ourselves down the river.

"It is. It's peaceful."

"Better than being at work?" I turn over my shoulder, still slightly ahead of him, rowing down the water. I can feel the sun beating down on my back, and the tightness of my skin tells me I didn't put on enough sunscreen. I can't bring myself to care right now, though, with the gentle waters lapping against my kayak rhythmically, lulling me into a serene state. A few ducks flap in the water nearby, and I gesture toward them as we talk.

"Way better. Thanks for stealing me."

He paddles up next to me so we are in line, drifting down the river.

"So how are we getting back once we get out of the river? How are we getting back to your truck?" Alex asks.

I shake my head. "Always such a planner, huh? Relax. I got it covered. Dane agreed to drive my truck out to West Bend, which is a few miles down. His mom will pick him up. We'll get out there and be able to drive back."

"You thought of everything," he says, smiling.

"Of course. I might be spontaneous and outdoorsy, but I'm not an idiot."

"Never said you were. I think you're amazing."

"Why thanks. I'm glad you noticed," I tease, lifting my oar to splash him.

"Don't start a fight you can't win," he jokes, splashing me back. For a long moment, we are two children engaged in a water battle in the middle of the river. I shriek and try to paddle away, but he's fast, catching on to the whole kayak scene way too quickly—this is his first time, he's informed me.

Before I can speed away or retaliate, though, the inevitable happens.

My kayak flips.

I hurriedly right myself, but not before getting a mouthful of dirty river water. When I emerge, gasping for air, my hair is matted to my face. I part it to get oriented.

"Marley, are you okay?" Alex asks, paddling toward me. I look at him, exhaling loudly.

"Just peachy," I tease. I try to wring out my hair without moving too much, trying not to tip the kayak. I touch the top of my head and realize my hat's gone. "Shit," I say.

Wordlessly, Alex scans the water, then paddles forward and scoops up my floating hat with his oar. "Saved the day," he says, handing me my hat.

"Hardly," I joke.

I settle myself back into the kayak, readjusting my now sopping-wet self. "You're going to pay for that."

"What, are you challenging me to another round?" he asks, raising an eyebrow and his oar.

"Don't push me. You'll regret it."

He stares at me wordlessly as we drift down the river, both paddling to keep the kayaks somewhat together.

"I don't think I could regret anything with you, Marley Jade." His voice is serious now, all the boyish playfulness gone. Despite my soaking wet hair and the overpowering smell of river water, I sober, too.

I stare at the man in the kayak beside me, the man I kidnapped today on a whim. I stare at the man who makes me feel like writing poetry, who makes me feel like kayaking on a Wednesday. I stare at the man who makes me feel like Rosewood might not be a dead end after all.

Looking up the river, I smile even more. "Look at that. We're almost at the exact point where you rescued me," I say, hardly believing it's only been three weeks. It feels like a lifetime ago. I feel like a different Marley.

He looks forward, eyeing the bridge. I wait for him to make a snarky, joking comment, but he doesn't. Instead, he paddles closer to me, holding on to the side of my kayak when I'm within reach. I stare, not sure what's happening.

"That was the scariest, craziest night of my life when you fell off that bridge. I thought I'd imagined you. But Marley, as weird as it sounds, it was also one of the best nights. Because if you hadn't fallen, I would've maybe never known you."

My heart flutters as we float underneath the bridge that changed it all, twice in my life.

Alex leans in slightly, and I lean to meet him in the middle. Life's about to change again, I think to myself. And it's at the same bridge.

Imagine….

And then it happens again.

***

There's a clinking of kayaks, a flailing of body parts, a hitting of my head on something. This time when I'm submerged, it's not an easy flip maneuver that rights me, because with Alex and his kayak so close, I'm bumping into too many obstructions.

When I kick free of my kayak and surface, I'm

gasping again, clinging to the floating kayak and trying to get my bearings. I'll never get used to being dunked in the water.

Alex comes up from the water sputtering and coughing, also clinging to his overturned kayak. "What the hell happened?" he asks, out of breath.

"I don't know. I think maybe I leaned too far?"

Realizing we're both safe, we calm down, still clinging to the kayaks, smiles now painting themselves on our faces. "Of all places," Alex says. "I almost had to save you again."

My mouth opens. "Me? You were the one who wasn't coming up for air. I thought I was going to have to save you."

"Please. I was a lifeguard. I'm a pro," he teases.

I raise an eyebrow. "Well, the almost kiss that didn't happen says otherwise."

"You're the one who flipped us."

"I think it was your fault. Who the hell tries to pull off a kiss in kayaks?"

Alex shrugs, making his way around his kayak toward me, both of us still bobbing in the river. He gets close enough to pull me to him, our kayaks awkwardly clinking at the ends. His free arm wraps around my shoulders, pulling me close. We're nose to nose, and I almost gasp, not from a lack of oxygen this time, but from the feeling of being this close.

"A man who finally is breaking free," he answers. It's an odd statement, but what's odder is that I get it.

111

Looking into his eyes, I don't see the same Alex from a few weeks ago or, hell, from a few days ago. I see a freer Alex, a passionate Alex.

I see a kissing-on-the-kayaks Alex.

Before I can analyze too much, his lips are on mine, and suddenly the gross river water disappears. I drown in his lips, in the feel of his tongue swirling effortlessly on mine. I feel a glow within that seems to burst outward, my head drowsy with a feeling I hadn't anticipated.

The kiss is slow and lingering, and even though we're still bobbing in murky water, it's not awkward or uncomfortable. It's like his lips were made for mine, or vice versa. It's like I've finally found the lips to complete me or undo me. Or maybe both.

Under the bridge where I fell not long ago, I fall yet again. But this time, I don't crash into the water, and I don't almost sink to the bottom.

This time, I float on the surface, crashing into a heart I'm only just beginning to uncover.

This time, it's not really Alex who saves me. I think this time, our lips still locked, our hearts beating wildly, we save each other.

***

By the time we finally get to our exit point from the river, we're both exhausted from the exertion—the physical exertion of kayaking and righting them after our fall, and the mental exhaustion of the revelations that happened here.

When we get out of the river, we're both sopping wet but smiling like fools. I guess that's how you know you did your first kiss right.

Alex loads both kayaks in the back as I start the truck. Dane's left a note on my seat.

Saw the picnic basket in the back. Ate a sandwich and stole the bottle of wine. Figured you at least owed me that.

"Dammit, Dane," I say aloud as Alex circles around to get into the truck.

"What's wrong?"

"Well, we did have a picnic lunch. But now, apparently, we only have one sandwich left and no wine. What an asshole." I slam my hands on the steering wheel, mad that our perfect date is no longer so perfect.

Alex grins. "Well, at least he got the truck here. I can't imagine making my legs walk back the whole way carrying the kayak. Anyway, it's not a big deal. Why don't we just get some takeout or something?"

"Sounds good," I agree, realizing nothing can get me down. Not even an asshole friend-slash-boss who stole my expensive bottle of wine.

Okay, by expensive, I mean it cost more than my usual eight-dollar bottle. But still.

"Your place or mine?" he asks.

I think about Mom and how she's probably home.

I'm not ready to face that meeting yet. I'm not ready for this afternoon to be tainted by whatever mood she's in.

"Yours okay?"

"Sure. But I'll warn you, it's a bachelor pad to the extreme."

"Okay. Fair warning. We can call in some food when we get there. Sound good?"

"Perfect," he says, and I head off in the direction of his apartment, thinking maybe the whole destroyed picnic lunch won't be so bad after all.

***

Sitting on his sofa in a pair of Alex's sweatpants and a T-shirt, I scarf down my lo mein as he eats his sesame chicken. We went with Chinese for today, and I'm glad. Screw Dane. He can have the nasty sandwich I made. This is one hundred times better.

I try not to think about how easily these sweatpants would come off, though, or how I'm not wearing a bra underneath this thick cotton shirt—it was soaking wet, and I didn't want to go home to grab clothes. I readjust myself on the tan couch, the only piece of furniture in the living room other than the television. Bachelor pad doesn't really describe it. It's more like extreme minimalism.

"So," Alex says between bites. "This is pretty good Chinese food. For a small town and all."

"I'm sure you have a million great restaurants where

you're from."

"At least. We've got quite a few Chinese restaurants to pick from."

"I bet it's so fun living in California." I twirl some lo mein on my chopstick. It's the only way to eat Chinese food, after all.

"It's definitely different. But it's the same, too." Alex takes a bite of chicken off his fork. He disagrees with my chopstick theory.

I shrug. "I'd love to see it someday."

"California?"

"Yep. And then some. I just wish I could see more. I feel like I'm missing so much, you know? I love it here, I do. But I just feel like there's a big world out there."

"So go see it. Promise yourself you'll do it." He stares right at me, his blue eyes piercing into me. He makes me want to say yes. He makes it sound possible.

But then I sigh, reality kicking in. "It's not easy."

"You keep saying that, Marley. But life isn't easy. Still, if you put off stuff because it isn't easy, then what the hell are you doing anyway?"

"I don't really know. That's the thing."

"Well, you've got time to figure it out. What about your writing? Have you been working on more poems?"

I grin. "Yeah. Seems like I have myself a new muse."

"And it seems like I have myself a new distraction. I still can't believe you convinced me to play hooky."

"We all need a break."

115

"You're right. It's good to be away. And I've had an amazing time."

"Other than almost drowning in gross river water?" I ask.

"Even with that. I'm serious. Thank you for reminding me vitamin D isn't a bad thing."

"Is that the only thing I reminded you about?" I tease, eyeing him coyly.

"Well, among other things." He puts his plate on the floor, reaching for mine. My heart flutters again. He leans toward me.

"I might be falling for you," he says.

"I might have already fallen for you. Literally and figuratively," I whisper as he leans in. I use my finger to swipe at a speck of sauce on his face, staring into his deep blue eyes.

"Are you okay with that? Falling for a square doctor like me?" he asks, now almost on top of me.

I look up at him. "You betcha," I respond, and then he takes my lips with his again, and I melt into the sofa, the Chinese food abandoned and forgotten.

Chapter Eleven

Marley

"So, how was your hot and steamy night?" Dane asks me when I stroll into Georgia's the next morning for my shift.

I raise an eyebrow. "You know, you *are* my boss. Most bosses wouldn't feel comfortable talking to their employees about their steamy dates."

He works on stacking some new coffee cups before the morning rush. "And most bosses don't drive a truck out for the convenience of their employees when they're on their hot date. Most bosses also don't live in a town with about 4.5 people where they can hear all the gossip about how their employee didn't go home the night before."

"True, I suppose. But last night was great."

"That's it? Great? You spend the night with Rosewood's newest, most eligible bachelor, and you can only use the word 'great' to describe it?"

"Jesus, I didn't think I was on a reality television show here. I know there isn't much privacy in Rosewood, but we could at least pretend to have some semblance of respect for a girl's private life."

"Marley Jade, do not use the Lord's name in that way."

I turn to face Mrs. Pearson, Rosewood's most active church member. She's swinging by for her extra early cup of coffee before heading to the church to pray for the souls of Rosewood, most of all probably mine. I wince.

"Sorry, Mrs. Pearson, got ahead of myself."

"It's okay, darling. What are you two talking about, anyway?" she asks as Dane prepares her usual order.

Dane snickers behind me as I punch in the amount in the register. "Oh, just—"

"Just Marley's evening. She had a busy one," Dane says, laughing.

Great. How the hell—er, heck—am I going to talk my way through this one?

"Oh really. That's nice, dear. What were you up to?"

"Nothing really. Just… well, nothing."

Dane hands Mrs. Pearson her coffee as I breathe deeply, trying to get my face to cool down.

"Hm," she hums, taking the coffee and handing me the exact amount. "Funny. Because I heard you spent the night at the handsome new doctor's apartment."

I bite my lip and shrug. What am I supposed to say to that? Damn Rosewood and its small-town, privacy-invading atmosphere.

Mrs. Pearson waits for a response, but I just say, "Have a great day, Mrs. Pearson," with the biggest smile I can fake.

She sighs, shaking her head. "Marley Jade, I'll say an extra prayer for you and your soul this morning." And with that, she spins and marches out of Georgia's, the bells on the door rattling on her way out.

I slump over the counter. "This town is out of control. Seriously."

"You should've known your sleepover with the outsider would be big talk, especially considering Mrs. Gene lives in the same apartment building."

"Sometimes I swear this place is stuck in a time warp. Can we just get on with it already? People need lives or social media or something."

"So anyway, since word's out about your promiscuous ways," Dane says, winking as I shake my head, "tell me more. Are you and the hot doctor an official item, I'm guessing? Are you two running to the altar yet?"

"Okay, first, with all your talk about his hotness, I'm starting to worry I might have some competition."

Dane shrugs. "If I were gay and so were he, I'd go for it."

"There are a whole lot of ifs in that statement. Plus, you're assuming he would fall for a sarcastic, nosy ass such as yourself."

"You know, Marley, some employees wouldn't be

comfortable calling their boss an ass."

"Too bad I knew you before you were my boss, you remember, back when you used to call me Bob Marley and trip me every chance you got in the hallway."

"Okay, anyway, we're getting off topic."

"There's nothing more to say. Besides, nothing scandalous happened. We ate Chinese food, watched a movie, and that was it. I fell asleep on his couch."

Dane raises an eyebrow as some of the morning regulars come in. "Really? You expect me to believe that?"

"You make it sound like I'm a sex-starved maniac." At that, Mr. Cory startles. I didn't realize he'd made his way to the counter. He walks very, very slowly. "Sorry, Mr. Cory. The usual?"

The ninetysomething man just nods, and I tell him his total.

"I just can't believe you'd miss an opportunity like that," Dane admonishes as he scurries about, picking up the slack for Becca, who is away at college now. Louise is sick, so it's just the two of us.

"I'm not going to rush into anything. Besides, we barely know each other. Not really."

"You know him well enough to blush every time he comes in. You know him well enough to take him kayaking and to spend every chance you get with him."

"Yeah, but what's the point? He's here for a few years, and then what? He's going to go back to California, and I'll be here, like I always am. I like him.

I do. But it seems kind of pointless to get all wrapped up in him when it can't work."

With the regulars all in their typical seats enjoying their usual orders, Dane touches my shoulder. I spin to look at him. "It's true, who knows where this thing between you will be in a few years. But don't you owe it to yourself to find out?"

"I think I owe it to myself to guard my heart," I say seriously.

"Marley Jade, since when do you play things so safe?"

"Since I've lost at love with basically every guy in this town. And since Alex Evans is too good for a girl like me. Look at me. What do I have to offer?"

Dane pauses, a serious look on his face. It's unfamiliar. He's never this serious. "You have a lot to offer, Marley, if you'd just stop holding yourself back from being happy. Stop trying to protect everyone else's happiness, and stop being so down on yourself. You're an amazing woman, and Alex will see that. You don't have to map out your whole life with him right now. Just see where this thing goes. Just be happy. And most of all, give yourself permission to find happiness for yourself, no matter what. You say you're not going anywhere, but the thing is, I don't think there's anything stopping you."

"Dane, you know why I can't just leave."

"That's the thing, Marley. I think you can. I think at some point you might have to. I think you should let go of clinging to the past and to your misplaced guilt. I think you have to let go and let yourself live a little. Because I think you've let Rosewood and its secrets hold you in too long."

I don't know how I feel about it all, but it does make me stop and think.

Being with Alex makes me feel so good. He makes me feel safe, yet also alive. He makes me want to dream big for the future, to think about a life beyond this town. He makes me want to be better, to live better, to live bigger.

Last night, kissing him on the sofa, I wanted to be all in. I wanted to let down the barbed wire around my heart and let go of all the rational reasons I should pull back. I wanted to succumb to him, to the man he is.

But I couldn't.

Because, just like every other man I've dared to fall for, I have a wall up. It's almost imperceptible, but it's there.

It's like no matter what I do, I won't let myself get too close because I know how this whole story ends.

It ends with him moving on to bigger, better things, and me standing in the shadow of Rosewood, just like the little girl who stood here wondering why bad things happen and realizing I could never leave behind all the things that happened here.

**

When my shift's over, I don't head to the oak tree to

do some writing like I want to. Instead, I head straight home. I need to check on Mom, make sure she made it out of bed and to work today. I tried to call earlier, but no one answered. I hope and pray this is a good sign.

When I round the corner and see our house, though, my heart sinks. Our car is in the driveway. Sometimes when Mom's really feeling good, she'll walk to work. Maybe today was just a good day.

Trudging through our front door, I toss my keys on the counter beside the stack of bills I still need to pay.

"Mom?" I yell, scanning the living room and kitchen for her. There's no answer.

I head down the hallway. Her door's still shut. I toss it back, fearing the worst but hoping for the best.

"Mom?" I yell again when I find her, sprawled on her back, her legs and arms spewing over the edges as she lies cockeyed in the bed.

I rush over and shake her, my heart pounding.

A groan from her tells me she's alive, but the empty bottle of Jack Daniel's beside her bed tells me she's far from okay.

Tears sting. How could I be such an idiot? How could I just leave last night, without even checking on her?

"Mom, are you okay?" I ask, knowing it's a ridiculous question.

Mom's never okay. She's never been okay.

"Get off. Leave me the fuck alone," she spews, her words choppy and lacking clear enunciation.

"Mom, I'm sorry," I say, tears falling now, the sight of her in this state bringing everything back.

I'm a horrible daughter. I should've stayed last night. I shouldn't have left her alone.

She rolls over, and I rush to the nightstand where I know there's Advil close by. Like I've done so many times, I reach for the bottle, popping out two.

I freeze, though, before handing them to her. There, beside the empty bottle, is the picture.

It's a smiling couple by the roller coaster where they met. She's kissing his cheek, youth radiating from them. It was taken one year after they met. It's where my dad proposed.

The picture makes me long for what once was but can never be again. They're happy. They're together. Mom's glowing and happy. The smile lines on her face tell me she's looking forward to the future. She's living life, she's free.

She's very different from the woman who is trashed in her bed at 2:00 p.m. on a weekday. She's very different from the woman who has been on her own emotional roller coaster for over a decade. She's nothing like that woman in the picture, a shell of the woman she could've been.

Shit. I'm a bigger idiot than I thought.

Yesterday. The date. September 1. It was their anniversary yesterday, the anniversary of when they met and also when he proposed. How could I be so selfish? How could I get so wrapped up in my own life that I forgot?

The familiar pang of guilt and pain throbs in my chest. I did this. It's my fault.

It's always my fault.

***

I sit on the sofa for the next few hours. I don't try to think about what to do or how bad I feel. I sit, a blank canvas, an empty shell, staring into the oblivion that's my life. I see my phone light up on the coffee table, the name "Alex" flashing on the screen. I ignore it. Over and over I ignore it.

Yesterday, everything was perfect. Yesterday, I thought maybe I could do it. Maybe I could let go of the guilt from the past. I could spread my wings a little, detach myself from the fucked-up situation that is my life.

But coming home, seeing Mom, remembering that I'm the only thread she has to keep it together, I realize I can't. How can I leave her here alone? How can I abandon her?

I can't. I simply can't.

A few hours later, there's a frantic knock on the door. I don't move, sitting in the blackness of the living room. I hear a key slide into the doorknob, and within minutes, Margaret's face is in front of me.

"Honey, I was worried. I saw your mom's car in the driveway all day. Is everything okay?"

I look up at her, my vision blurry from crying. "No."

125

Margaret nods. I don't have to say anything else. She knows. She's always known.

"It's going to be okay," she reassures like she's done so many times, patting me on the shoulder.

But for once in my life, I can't believe Margaret. I can't believe anything is ever going to be okay. For fourteen years, I've tried to believe it's going to sort itself out, that Mom's going to get better. For fourteen years, I've listened to her in her upswings tell me she's done with drinking, that she's going to move on.

For fourteen years, I've watched her wreck her life, the ghost of the man who left her clinging to her soul in ways I can't bear to understand.

And for fourteen years, all I could do is sit idly by, hoping I could save her from the fate my dad met, hoping I could be the link to salvation she needs.

For fourteen years now, I've felt like nothing but a failure, a letdown, and a disgrace.

For fourteen years, I've been stuck in this purgatory. And, despite Margaret's soft voice, when she walks back to check on Mom and try to make things better, I know there's no way out.

Chapter Twelve

Alex

I probably shouldn't be here, but it's too late to worry now. The door creaks open, and Marley faces me, the familiar red hat on her black hair.

But the Marley Jade smile I've come to know, the shrieking playful girl from a few days ago in the kayak, she's gone. The bridge Marley is back, the sad eyes Marley.

Dr. Conlan's right. Even if she's ignored my phone calls for days, even if she's tried to avoid me, she needs someone. I don't know if I can be that someone. I don't know what good I could possibly be. But looking at her, it's apparent she's going through hell.

We stare a long moment. I have no idea what's going on other than issues with her mom—Dr. Conlan told me I need to wait for Marley to tell me everything when she's ready. I know Marley's got her demons, but I'm starting to realize how deeply they run.

I don't know what to say or do, but I don't have to. I realize coming here is exactly what I should've done. Before I can second-guess myself or figure out what to say, she steps forward, falling into my arms, the smell of her perfume and the feel of her warm, soft skin beneath my fingers telling me I'm right where I belong and that, just like the night of the bridge, Marley just needs someone to pull her back.

Maybe, just maybe, I can be that person.

"Can we go for a walk?" I ask, and Marley nods, pulling the door shut behind her as we head off into the night.

***

"I'm sorry for just swinging by, but I got worried," I say quietly, Marley staring ahead as we walk the streets now familiar to me.

"I'm sorry for ignoring you. I just... it's been a rough few days."

I let the silence seep in between us, not wanting to push her too far.

"I've missed you," I declare, meaning it.

The past few days without Marley have shown me exactly what she's come to mean to me. Gone were the days of careless walks in Rosewood, cheesesteaks with Moe, or impromptu trips around town. Gone were the days of easy laughter. My days again settled into routine—work, sleep, eat, and study.

My dad would be proud, but my heart wasn't happy.

I was bored. I was drowning in monotony and loneliness.

We walk in silence, the night air crisp, the stars twinkling above us. We head to the park, Marley's favorite one. Wordlessly we sit on the bench, and she leans into me as we study the night sky.

"He used to bring me here," she starts, like a whispered prayer into the night.

I have an arm around her shoulders, and I gently play with the ends of her hair. I don't say anything, letting her go on at her own pace.

"He used to bring me here when I was a little girl on nights just like this. Mom would tell him it was crazy, that he shouldn't have a four-year-old out at this time of night. But he didn't care. He'd just smile and tell her we'd be back. We'd walk down here and sit, right here, and he'd point out stars. I, of course, had no idea what he was talking about, naming those shiny dots in the sky. I'd wriggle and fiddle and fidget, wanting him to finish his lesson so we could go swing like we always did. He loved the stars, though. He would always talk about how far away they are but how beautiful, how perfect."

She looks at me now as I study her. A tear slides down her cheek, and I reach up to wipe it away. But more tears fall, and I can't keep up.

"Alex, I love you. I know it's probably too soon and I know it's crazy. I know I'm just some plain girl from Rosewood, I'm just a stop in your amazing life. But I realized on that kayak that I love you so damn much it scares me."

It's an odd confession of love, in the middle of such sadness. It's like her emotions are running wild, yet, in truth, it's the most honest, genuine confession of love I can imagine. It feels real and natural. It's exactly what I needed to hear.

"I love you too. And you're not just some plain girl. You're not just a stop. You've reminded me what living is. I used to think life was about achieving, about climbing the ladder of success. I used to think life was eating three meals a day and studying and working. You've shown me in this past month that life is this, right here. I love you, too, Marley. And not just for now. Not just for a while. I love you for good." I lean in then, her tears still falling, and I kiss her.

This kiss is different. It's not the perfect, playful kiss from a few days ago. It's a real kiss, a kiss mixed with lingering doubts and fears. It's mixed with the pain she's feeling that I want so desperately to make disappear.

The kiss is soft and slow. I pull back to look at her, her soft cheeks in my hands.

She looks up at me. "I don't think this is going to work."

I pull back, confused. What the hell is she talking about? The rush from a few minutes ago of knowing she's feeling what I'm feeling stops. "What do you mean?"

"I can't do this. I can't lead you down this path with me. I just can't."

She turns her face away now, staring off to the left, into the distance. I get off the bench, kneeling in front of her, taking her hands in mine. I wait for her to look at me. "Marley, what's wrong? What are you talking about? Talk to me."

She swipes at her tears. "Alex, you're amazing. You're this perfect guy with a perfect life ahead of you. And I thought I could be the girl you needed. I thought maybe, just maybe, we could carve out a future together, that maybe the past was really over. But these last few days, I've realized I've been kidding myself. I told myself when I first met you to shut those feelings off, that I wasn't good enough for you. But then, I don't know, maybe it was love and the craziness of it, but I thought maybe, just maybe, we could work."

"We can work, Marley. I know it's scary and we have some stuff to figure out. But we have time. I'm on residency for a few years."

"But I don't want to suck you into all this. I'm not good for you."

"What are you talking about?"

"I'm talking about my baggage. My past. I'm fucked-up, Alex. My family is fucked-up, and so am I. I'm never going to be the woman I want to be, and I'm never going to be good for you."

"Hey, stop." I squeeze her hands.

"You don't understand," she says, shaking her head.

"Make me understand, then."

She wipes at her tears, taking a moment to try to compose herself. I stay put, kneeling in front of her, afraid if I move, it'll break her will to talk.

"I can't leave her. Ever. I can't leave my mom behind. She needs me."

"Okay. Then we'll stay here."

"I can't ask you to do that."

"You're not asking me. I'm telling you. If you need to stay here, we'll stay here. We'll figure it out. Like I said, we have time." I squeeze her hands again before lifting one to my lips and kissing the top of it, feeling surer of this than anything else.

She studies my eyes. "You need to know what you're getting into."

"Then tell me."

She nods, and, sensing I've finally gotten through to her, I take my seat beside her again, pulling her in close.

"My dad killed himself when I was seven. He'd been struggling with mental health issues. He was in this bad place. Mom tried to pull him out of it, tried to get him help. It didn't work. He killed himself on the Cedar Bend Bridge. Took a pistol, shot himself right there."

"Marley, I'm so sorry," I say, feeling her pain radiate through me.

She takes a deep breath. "Dr. Conlan and Margaret

were there for me. They tried to shield me from it all. They did. For a long time, I thought my dad had just died in an accident. But they couldn't shield me from the fact he was gone and that mom was falling apart. She sunk into a depression and eventually turned to alcohol. They sent her to rehab, and I lived with them for a while. She came back, and she seemed okay. But she wasn't. How could she be?"

I squeeze her to me, kissing the top of her head, my heart ravaged by her sadness. It's deeper than I thought. She continues.

"When I finally found out what happened to Dad, I was devastated. How didn't I know? Why didn't I do anything? Why couldn't I be enough for him to want to live? As an adult, I understand that I was only seven and couldn't be expected to shoulder that kind of weight. I know, deep down, I couldn't have stopped him. My dad was sick. He'd struggled with mental illness his whole life. But a part of me, that little girl in me, still wonders why I couldn't do anything."

"It's not your fault," I declare. The words feel cheap and too simple, but I don't know what else to say. My heart burns with a desire to fix this, but it also burns with the knowledge that I can't.

"I know. Rationally, I know. But I also know that Mom blames herself. Mom's come treacherously close many times to sinking into the same place my dad was. I vowed to myself I wouldn't let that happen. I couldn't save my dad because I was too young. But I can save my mom."

"That's a lot on your shoulders," I remark.

I see her jaw clench. "I can handle it. I have to."

"But you don't have to do it alone, Marley."

"I've had help. Margaret and Joe have been a godsend. They've been there every step, helping me, saving me on nights Mom was in a drunken rage. Margaret, in many ways, was the mother to me that Mom could never be. Mom's not easy, I realize that now. But I know it's not her fault. I know I can't blame her."

"Still. That's a lot of weight you've carried."

"I can handle it."

"And so can I," I vow now, turning her chin to me. "I can handle it all, too. Let me handle it with you. Let me be there for you."

"But how can I let you? How can I drag you into this mess with me?"

"You're not dragging me anywhere. I love you, Marley. All of you. Everything that made you who you are. When I look at you, I don't see baggage or a broken woman. I see a survivor. I see strength. And I see beauty. Not just physical beauty, but emotional. You make life worth living. You make life exciting. I want a piece of that with you, no matter what that looks like. I want to help you find happiness, too. I want to help you find a version of your dreams, no matter what it takes. Let me be there for you."

She's breathing hard now, like she's at a crossroads,

a pivot point. My heart beats fast, wondering if I've gotten through.

She looks at me, for a long time, and it's like I can see the past Marley, the pained Marley, coming to terms with the current woman she is.

"Okay, Alex Evans. Okay."

"Okay, then," I agree, and I kiss her again.

Chapter Thirteen

Alex

"So, where are we going?" Marley asks when I pick her up after her shift at Georgia's on Friday.

"You'll see. Trust me," I say.

She raises an eyebrow and pretends to scowl, but I can see the smile behind it.

"You have your journal, right?" I ask. I only texted her three times today to remind her. Without it, this whole plan is going to fall apart.

Not that it might not fall apart anyway. I'm still a little nervous. But nothing risked, nothing gained, and all that cliché business. We all have to go outside of our comfort zone now and then, and I think Marley just needs a shove.

"Yes, but I'm a little worried." She tosses her apron onto the counter and waves to Evelyn as we leave Georgia's, walking into the starry night.

"Don't be. It's a good thing."

She wraps herself around my arm like she always does, her free hand swinging. We trudge along, my hands in my faded jeans, my official "date night" button-up on.

"You need to undo a button. You look too... stuffy," she remarks, stopping me on the sidewalk to undo two buttons.

I reach down and claim her lips, kissing her as she clutches my shirt. I pull back. "We need to go so we're not late."

"So let's go then," she says, grinning, kissing my neck down, down....

"If you keep that up, we're not going to move past this square on the sidewalk."

"Well, we might want to take it somewhere else. Officer Randy is no joke when it comes to indecent exposure," she whispers in my ear, her lips close, making me struggle to contain a groan.

I pull back, yank on her hand. "Come on. Let's go. I don't want to ruin your surprise."

She raises an eyebrow. "Whatever you say, doctor boy. Have it your way."

I lead her to my Chevy, which I've managed to sort of clean out in preparation for tonight. There's a grocery bag of empty water bottles, Gatorades, and Dorito bags. But hey, at least they're contained... sort of.

As soon as she hops in, she flips the radio to the pop station, puts her feet on the dash, and starts singing.

"You know you shouldn't ride with your feet up," I say.

"Relax. It's fine," she argues, rolling down her window to stick her arm out. I shake my head. This girl's a disaster waiting to happen.

But I take a deep breath and remind myself to relax. That's just Marley for you. Free, wild, and a little reckless. It's not always a bad thing to live on the edge a little.

I guess.

We drive for twenty minutes, Marley constantly asking how much longer and begging me to tell her the surprise.

I pull up to the swanky little bar, Delilah's. I found it online. It's exactly what Marley needs, what we need.

"What are we doing here? You brought me to a bar?" she asks, smiling, her eyes questioning me.

"You'll see. Just come on," I say, unbuckling my seat belt. We're only five minutes early. We don't have a lot of time.

Marley unbuckles her belt and hops out. I walk around the car to take her hand and then lead her to the door.

Inside, a smoky jazz singer is belting out a song into the microphone on the stage up front. There are a few tables with couples sitting and a few people at the bar. It's not too crowded, but that's okay. It'll be the perfect way to ease her in.

We head to the bar and I turn to her. "Iced tea," she

says.

The bartender eyes me. "Same."

We get a condescending look, but I ignore it, handing over a ten and taking our iced teas to an empty table up front.

The jazz singer, in the meantime, finishes her song, and a woman heads to the mic, clapping furiously.

She's got permed hair that's bigger than life itself and a bright, neon-orange dress on. She's laughing and clapping. "Thanks so much, Martha. Wasn't that just astounding? Gorgeous. Wow. So I see some new faces, and I'm excited about that. Thanks for coming to our monthly poetry reading. I'm excited to see support for the arts," she says.

Marley turns to me and grins. "A poetry reading? Cool." She turns back to the stage, and she looks entranced.

"So as many of you know, my mother was an aspiring poet. When she died last year, I thought it would be a neat way to pay tribute to her and to give some budding poets a platform if we started a monthly poetry night. Tonight, we welcome several new poets to the mic. First up, we have Bradley Jonas. Let's give him a warm Delilah's welcome."

I put my iced tea down, clapping for Bradley. Marley puts her hands up to clap wildly. The bar is empty, but the excitement is palpable. I've never been to a poetry reading—not quite my thing—but I find I'm excited, too.

Of course, it may be because Marley's eating this up. And I hope to hell the sentiment continues, because I'm not done with her yet.

***

When Bradley is done with his poem, I feel the sweat beading. His sonnet or ballad or whatever the hell it was seemed to take forever.

My palms are so sweaty, I wipe them on my jeans, knowing what's coming out of Delilah's mouth next as her permed hair bounces back up to the mic. "Wow. Just wow, Bradley. Thank you. And next, we need to give a warm welcome to our latest poet to be joining us. She's from Rosewood and works at one of my favorite coffee spots around. Let's give a warm welcome to Marley Jade."

The crowd claps, and so do I. Marley doesn't, though. She freezes, staring at the mic. Then, slowly, she turns her head to face me, eyes huge.

"What the hell?"

My stomach lurches. I try to sell it, though. "You've got this. Just go for it."

"No way. I can't."

I stare, the fearless Marley at a loss for words. The go-get-it girl is stuck, freaking out, and drowning.

I reach across the table for her hand. The crowd's trying to keep the clapping going, but it's fading. Delilah just stands at the mic as it makes the signature screech from feedback.

"You've got this. It's time for you to go after your dreams," I assure her.

"I've never shared anything before. I'm not very good," she hisses at me.

"I don't believe it, Marley. Don't think about it. Just go do it. Go after your dream. What do you have to lose?"

"What if I blow it?"

"You won't. And if you do, I'm right here. Just look at me. Just read your poem to me."

She contemplates the scene for a moment. Finally, very carefully, she digs her journal out of her bag. She trudges to the stage as if she's on a death march, one foot painfully placed in front of the other, her head unmoving as she stares straight ahead. She stiffly stands before the mic, her face pale.

"Hello, I'm Marley Jade. I've never done this sort of thing, ever. I'm sorry if you hate it."

The crowd chuckles and murmurs a little bit.

"Okay," she says, flipping through her journal until she finds the one she wants. I don't take my eyes off her. This is it. This is the moment I've been waiting for, the moment she's been waiting for but didn't know it.

"It's called 'The Rose.'"

And then, Marley Jade reads her poem.

When she finishes her reading, she stares, and the crowd is silent. She bites her lip, readjusts her hat, and walks off stage, head down.

A clap begins from the back, and slowly, surely, all

hands are slapping together in the bar. I find myself leaping to my feet, and a few others do the same. We clap for the beauty of a budding poet finding herself right before us. We applaud for the truth that something's shifted before us. As she makes her way back to the table, I hug and kiss her.

"You did it. You were amazing," I whisper, kissing her cheek.

I pull back to see tears in her eyes, Marley clutching her journal. "I can't believe I did it. I can't believe you did this for me. Thank you."

And I know at that moment, the risk was worth it.

***

When we leave Delilah's, there's a silence between us in the car, like we both know something has shifted for her.

"Thank you again. That was the best night of my life," she whispers.

"You betcha," I say, smiling at her, glad things worked out. "Your poem was intense and beautiful."

"Thank you." There's a pause as she glances at me. "I wrote it for my dad."

"I thought maybe you did. It was a beautiful tribute."

"He was a beautiful man, even though he had his demons. I hate him sometimes for what he did, but I don't. I know I can't understand what he had to deal with."

I pull out of the parking spot and head back toward Rosewood. Reaching down, I turn the knob on the radio to turn it down, wanting the appropriate atmosphere for what I'm about to ask.

"Can I ask you something serious?" I venture, a little nervous again.

"Of course."

"That night. On the bridge."

I glance over at her as we stop at the stop sign.

She nods. "Go on."

"Were you…. I mean… what were…."

"You want to know if I was trying to kill myself?" she asks solemnly.

"I'm sorry, Marley. I know you said you weren't. It's not that I don't trust you—"

"It's fine, Alex. It's a fair question. But the answer is no. Truly, no. I'm not going to say I haven't ever thought about it over the years, because there were dark days. But no. I saw what happened in the aftermath of my father's suicide. I saw what it did to those who loved him. I couldn't do it."

"I'm sorry."

"Don't be. You had something you needed to ask. Don't apologize for that."

"What were you doing out there then?"

She shrugs, taking a moment to answer. "Sometimes, when things are getting intense, I go out there. I sit where he sat. I guess I just feel like maybe it's where I can feel close to him. I don't feel him at his grave. I guess I just want to get perspective, to see what he saw last."

"What about the bag?"

"It was alcohol." She says it as if it's a simple fact.

"Oh." I'm not sure what else to say.

"I wasn't getting drunk, if that's what you're thinking. I take it with me because the only thing I remember about my dad was that he liked drinking Jack Daniel's. It's like a weird tribute. I also take it because it's also my mom's drink of choice when she's going on a bender. I take it to remind myself how messed up it can make you. I take it as kind of a fuck you to the universe, like a go ahead and throw your best shot at me. I'm not biting."

"I see." And I sort of do.

"You don't." I glance over at her, but there's no anger on her face. Just the Marley smile. "It's okay. How could you? You're from a different world, Alex. A different life. And I don't begrudge you that. It's just, there are some things you'll probably never understand about me. I'm okay with that."

"I want to understand."

"I know. And I hope in time you will. But a part of me is also afraid if you truly understand, completely, you won't want to understand anymore. I'm a little scared, Alex. More scared than when I walked on that stage tonight, and let me tell you, I was freaking scared."

"You don't have to be scared about me. I love you. All of you."

I reach for her hand and pull it to my lips, letting them linger for a moment too long.

"I love you too."

We drive the rest of the way to her house in a silence befitting the mood, the moment, and the revelations we've just experienced.

Chapter Fourteen

Marley

He's in this for real.

We're pulling up to the house, and I literally have to bite my lips to keep myself from smiling like a clown. From the poetry surprise to his words on the way home, I just have to pinch myself. This is real life. Alex Evans loves me. I just read one of my poems in front of a crowd. Life is going somewhere.

I'm happy. Truly, madly happy.

"Can I walk you in?" he asks.

I turn to see Mom's car in the driveway. My heart sinks. "I don't know if that's such a good idea. Mom's home."

"Don't you think it's time I meet her?"

"I don't know. She's…."

"Marley Jade, there's nothing that could happen, there's nothing that could make me change my mind. I know things are rough in your life. I know things aren't smooth. I'm ready for that. I'm ready to face it, head-on. Let me in. Let me understand."

I stare into those perfect blue eyes, eyes I'm learning can get me to say and do anything.

"Okay," I whisper, although inside, I'm screaming no. But if things are going to get ugly, if Alex is going to go running, better now than later. Might as well get it over with, let him see the whole truth.

Walking up to the door, I hold my breath. Every other guy I've brought home has pretty much known the story, has known my history. They've known how screwed-up my family is when they got involved.

Of course, the guys I dated before didn't care. They were of a different lot than Alex. I lead him up the path to the door, squeezing his hand.

"You ready?"

"More than."

I open the door and lead Alex completely and fully into my world.

***

"Mom, I'm home," I yell, wondering where we'll find her. I lead Alex in and leave him in the kitchen as I traipse down the hallway. I don't make it far. Mom comes staggering down the hallway to the main living area. Her half-closed eyes, her clumsy gait, and her frizzy hair tell me everything I need to know.

There'll be no hiding the truth from Alex tonight, no sugarcoating things. He's going to get the entire mucky picture.

"Where the fuck have you been?" Mom shouts, slurring her words.

"Mom, sit down. Here, let me help you."

She shoves me. "Get the hell off, you fucking slut. Who's this?" She motions toward Alex, and my gut drops. This was a horrible idea. I'm an idiot. I turn to see Alex, hands in his pockets. He's stoic, not moving, but I can see his jaw clenching.

"Hi, Ms. Jade. I'm Alex Evans."

"Well look at that. Alex Evans. What a pretty boy you've got, Marley. Did you fuck him yet?"

"Mom, that's enough. We're leaving." Tears sting my eyes.

"Good. Go. I don't need you anyway. You think I need you here? You think you're doing any good here? Go off with him. Good luck to you, Alex. She's a slutty waste of life. Going nowhere."

"Mom, stop. It's the alcohol. It's the alcohol talking," I say, tears flowing now. I know, deep down, it's the alcohol, but it doesn't make it hurt any less.

"Don't tell me what it is and what it isn't. Get out. Don't fucking come back," she screams, and Alex heads toward me, wrapping me in his arms.

Mom staggers up the hall, murmuring and muttering.

I cry freely into Alex's chest. I should be used to this. It's nothing new. But the sting of embarrassment hurts even more. I look up at him, at a loss for words. I look in his eyes, expecting to see judgment or horror.

I don't see either. I just see empathy and understanding. He pulls me closer.

I try to say I'm sorry, but the words don't come out. Despite the look on his face, I'm terrified. I'm petrified he's going to go running, to retract those words. This might be when Alex sees I'm truly broken, that the sunshine, go-get-life Marley is kind of a fraud.

I'm not completely the carefree woman I want to be. I can try and try, but I can't be. Life's shit on the idea too many times. No matter how much I try to appreciate life and to live it, I can't, not in the way I want.

Alex doesn't run away, though, and he doesn't even look scared. He whispers, "Come home with me, Marley. You don't have to stay."

I look up at him, at those eyes I've come to trust. I glance down the hall at the doorway where my mother is, thinking about how much I've sacrificed in this life for her, because of her.

So I do what I haven't been able to do yet, even though I should have a long time ago.

I nod, take Alex's hand, and I leave. My mother will have to handle her own messes tonight, and she'll have to realize this girl might not be here forever to take care of her and her problems.

I love my mom despite everything. I love her even when she can't love me back. I do. But sometimes you need to let go, you need to make your own way, and you need to do something that scares you a little.

***

On the way to Alex's, I call Margaret like I've done so many times before. She asks if I need a place to stay, but I tell her I'm fine. I ask if she and Joe can check on Mom sometime. I feel bad, but I know there's no sense in trying to get through. When Mom's in this mood, it's best to stay out of her way. The guilt creeps in for leaving, but I try to suffocate it. I'm doing the best I can. I've done the best I can.

I can't keep fighting this fight.

We get to Alex's apartment, and he leads me inside. Suddenly, the butterflies are back.

"I'm sorry you had to see all that," I start again, apologizing for the tenth time.

"Shh," he whispers, shushing me and kissing my cheek. "You have nothing to apologize for. You're not your mother. You can't be responsible for everything she does. I'm just sorry you have to endure that. It can't be easy."

I shrug. "It's nothing new. She'll sober up tomorrow, and it'll be normal for a while. She needs help, but there's no convincing her. I've tried."

"I know you have. But you can't shoulder this alone. Your mom has to want to get better, Marley. You can't save her from herself, no matter how hard you try."

I look up at his face, his arms wrapped around me. For the first time in my life, I feel like I can buy that. I feel like maybe he's right.

I don't owe anyone an apology for who my mother

is. I don't owe my life for her. And I can't make her want to change. I can't make her want to live.

Most of all, I can't make her love me, no matter how much I want to.

"Tonight is about you. What you did out there on that stage was amazing, Marley. Own it. Relish it. Don't let anything take away from it. You're amazing. You deserve to pursue this poetry thing. You deserve to see it through. You deserve to be happy," he says, leaning in and taking my lips in his.

The kiss feels so right, but I can't ease the tension I'm feeling.

Alex, the kiss, being here—this isn't what I expected. Sure, I've been attracted to Alex since day one. Sure, I've realized he gets me, he completes me in ways I didn't think possible.

But there's so much broken in me. There's such a lack of trust, and there's such a fear. What if this all falls apart? What if I'm not good enough for him? What if I bring disaster to his life?

I pull back for a moment before things can go to the point of no return. "Listen, Alex. I'm not the person you think I am, not completely. I'm not all wild and carefree. I'm not all okay. I'm a little bit broken, a little bit undone. I'm scared of life sometimes, and I'm scared of who I'll become." The silence between us seems to construct a wall. I feel a new distance. I feel myself putting the wall up.

"Aren't we all?" He kisses my hand, gently,

smoothly, as if I'm a princess who's earned the love of her knight. I'm hardly the sort. I pull back slightly, wanting him to hear every word clearly.

"Maybe. But I don't want you being fooled. I'm not the perfect woman. But the thing is, despite that, despite my flaws, I've realized I want you anyway. I want you to love me anyway."

"I can't do that," he says, and my heart freezes. I'm not surprised, though. I knew this could happen, probably should happen. I'm not the woman who deserves him.

He takes a step closer, bridging the gap between us. He takes my hand again, and his touch soothes my nerves. "I can't love you anyway. I can't love you despite your imperfections. But I can love you because of them. Marley, I don't want perfection. Hell, what does that even mean? I want you, every single piece of you, every undone and scarred and broken piece. I want the parts of you that are whole and the parts that are incomplete. I want all of you, Marley. I just want you."

With that, I succumb to the kiss he plants on my lips. I succumb to the consumption of my breath, my lips, by his. His mouth moves over mine, and I give in, his tongue finding mine and swirling in the knowledge that we are undeniably all-in.

He steps forward, pushing me backward, down the hallway. My feet scuttle over the shaggy carpet, plush under my toes as we inch toward his bedroom. Already, he's undoing my dress, and my hands are finding his belt, unbuckling it as we greedily grasp at each other, the burning desire within me now an unquenchable fire.

When we get to the bed, I let my dress fall, over my hips, crinkling into a heap on the floor as he finishes shedding his pants and yanks his shirt over his head. We are not calm or shy about it, driven by raw instinct and passion that won't quit.

As quickly as he can, he finds my lips again, kissing me until I feel like I can't breathe, until I feel like I need him just so I can survive.

He eases me onto the bed, covering my body with his, pulling back only to look into my eyes.

"I love you, Marley Jade. All of you."

"I love you, too," I whisper as his hands find my wrists, putting my arms over my head and claiming me as his own as he covers my mouth with his again.

He explores my body, kissing his way down as my heart races with every touch of his lips. The aching longing within me makes it undoubtedly clear; every piece of me is his to do what he will with it. Although I'm still a little scared, I give in, all in, to the truth within me.

I may be all his, but he's also all mine. He doesn't let me forget it as we give in to the longings within, exploring each other and giving to each other in ways we never imagined possible that black night on the bridge.

Chapter Fifteen

Marley

When Alex leaves for his shift the next morning, I don't rush off like I normally would in this type of situation. Instead, I linger a little longer between his plain white sheets, wrapped in his Star Wars comforter in the unfamiliar room that feels so familiar now.

I roll onto my back, smiling at the ceiling, thinking about how, despite everything, I'm lucky.

Last night was the single best night of my life, despite my mom's outburst. It's crazy how even during that, I found happiness.

It makes me feel like maybe, just maybe, happiness isn't forever gone. Maybe Alex can help me find it and keep it. Maybe it's here to stay.

I think about staying in Alex's bed until he gets home—I'm off work today. I think about what it would be like to just stay here, to never go back. I fantasize about the freedom, the not having to tiptoe around and worry about where she is or what she's going to do next.

But then the guilt comes banging at my door. I would still worry. I would feel guilty. I can't just disappear, no matter how much I want, even if she wants me to.

Sighing, I traipse to Alex's shower and make do with the limited man products he has. I wash away the beauty of last night, the connection, and realize as the cold, drafty air of the apartment slaps my skin that I'm back to reality.

I've washed away last night. I've washed away the dream that this right here could be my life.

And I do what I always do. I go crawling back to check on her, to see how she is. I abandon my smile to help her find hers.

***

She's sitting at the table when I go home, stirring a bowl of oatmeal. The bags under her eyes and her messy hair tell me she's feeling it this morning like she always does.

"You're back," she says, her voice the gravelly one I recognize.

"Yeah."

There's a long silence as I stare at her, waiting to see what she remembers. Waiting to see if she remembers.

"I was awful to you last night, wasn't I?" she asks.

I nod.

"I'm sorry."

"It's fine."

A lie. The lie I've told so many times before. Still, the air somewhat cleared between us, I head over to the coffeepot to make some.

"I'm going to take a shower before work. Will you be home later?" she asks.

I turn to look at her, studying her.

Pitying her.

This has become her normal. This, a messy hair, oatmeal, and shower kind of day has become her new high. It's a good day because she's managed to get out of bed.

It's a good day because she's said she's sorry, and life will go on like it has. This is what I've come to hope for, what I've come to expect. This is the reality we've both settled for.

I don't think it's good enough. Alex has made me realize this isn't good enough.

"I don't think so, Mom."

She doesn't say anything. The apathy I've come to know settles between us as she sloshes her oatmeal around before spooning a heaping tablespoon into her mouth. I wait, like I have for years, for something, anything.

Instead, Mom shoves her mouth full of oatmeal, and I shove the falsely placed hopes right back down where they belong.

***

"Come on, didn't' you tell me we should live a little? It's not that different than kayaking," Alex coaxes, as I finally shrug and take my T-shirt off, the red bikini top the only cloth between me and him.

"Fine. But I still think it's too chilly for swimming in the lake."

It's the beginning of October, and there's a definite bite in the afternoon air. The sun is out, and the temperature's high enough, but the hint of autumn seeps into my bones as I stand in cut-off shorts and a bikini top.

Alex is in some funky board shorts, his Chevy parked underneath a patch of trees by the lake.

We're about an hour from Rosewood for this adventure, which was Alex's idea. I smile, thinking about how not long ago, I was the adventurer. Now he's taken the wheel, always finding something new for us to explore, usually outdoors.

"I've created a monster," I say as I unbutton my shorts. He's not listening though, intently staring at my fingers as I wriggle my hips and let the shorts fall.

"In many ways," he responds, grinning at me, stepping forward to pull me in tight. He starts kissing my neck, and I giggle.

"Stop, we're here to swim."

"I'm good at multitasking. I do have the doctors' touch."

"Oh my God," I exclaim, pretending to be annoyed. "Stop. Just stop. Get the hell in the water. It was your grand idea to come swimming. So dammit, we're swimming," I argue.

It's a Wednesday, so this part of the lake is pretty barren. Not many people have ventured out to the lake in the middle of an October week. It's peaceful, only the sounds of nature here.

I pull on his hand and run toward the water, yanking him in after me.

"I'm not going to have to rescue you today, am I?" he asks, and I roll my eyes.

"Okay, are you ever going to let that story go?" I ask as we head in past our knees.

"No way. It makes me sound heroic. Brave even."

"Okay, if you say so. It's not like I fell off the Golden Gate, you know."

We keep heading in, now up to our necks, treading the water near each other. I shiver a little, as does Alex.

"You might be right. It might be a little bit chilly," he admits, exhaling like you do in winter when you can see your breath. Of course, he's being a bit dramatic—it's not cold enough to make breath rings.

"Well, after our swim, I'm sure we can find a way to warm up," I say, winking and laughing.

"Okay, I thought you told me we were here to swim? You tease," he accuses, giving my bottom a gentle slap under the water.

"You like it."

"I'm not arguing."

"It's so pretty here," I remark, looking around.

"I can't believe I've never been."

"Well, I'm glad we get to experience it together. I can't wait to experience even more. I can't wait to take you to California someday with me."

A few months ago, the thought of California would've scared me. The thought of Alex heading back without me terrified me, the prospect of leaving Rosewood not even in the realm of possibility.

But now, surrounded by the murky lake water and the beauty of this place, I smile. I can't wait to see more with Alex, too. I don't know how it's going to work yet. I don't know what it'll look like, and I'm not completely ready to dive in.

I'm not running from the idea, though, either. Looking at this gorgeous man in front of me, I think about how wonderful it would be to just jump into life with him, hand in hand, exploring every corner of this globe. I think about all the memories we could make, all the crazy adventures, all the laughs.

I keep treading water, pulling in closer to him now, though. "You know, I've been writing more."

"Really? That's awesome, Marley."

"Yeah. I'm thinking about going back to Delilah's next month. I've written three new poems. It's like I can't stop."

"I'm happy for you. That's amazing."

"It's all because of you."

"No way. I didn't do this. You did. You just needed a little shove." He pulls me to him in the water, our arms wrapped around each other.

"Well, regardless, thank you. I owe you."

He raises an eyebrow. "I'll take you up on that, you know."

"Don't be crass," I admonish, pretending to scowl.

"Don't be so damn sexy in a bikini beside me."

I try to think of a sexy comeback, playful banter, but I can't. The next thing I know, we're kissing in the middle of the lake, a picture-perfect autumn day around us.

When we finally pull away and swim to the shore, I don't think either of us is cold anymore.

"My place?" Alex asks as we scramble for our towels.

I shrug. "Your back seat cleaned out?"

"If you don't mind a few Dorito bags," he says, grinning.

"I happen to like Doritos," I retort, rushing toward the back seat, Alex right behind me.

"To new adventures," he says as we cram in.

"To new adventures," I echo, and succumb to his kiss, a few Dorito bags crinkling underneath me.

Chapter Sixteen

Alex

A few nights later, I hear a knock at the door as I'm eating my dinner—cereal.

Marley's working at Georgia's, so it can't be her. Who the hell else would be knocking?

I head to the door in my sweats and T-shirt, flinging back the door to see a shocking surprise.

"Dad, what are you doing here?" I ask, truly not expecting to see him.

He steps in the door. "Son. Good to see you, too."

"I'm just surprised is all. I wasn't expecting you." I step back, still holding my cereal bowl, truly shocked. I was not expecting this.

"That's the definition of a surprise, after all," he says, letting himself into my apartment, appraising my living quarters with a serious glance.

"So, what are you doing here?" I follow him in, setting the cereal bowl on my counter.

"I had to speak at a conference a few hours from here. I figured I'd pop by since I'm so close. I only have a few hours until I have to make my flight."

"That's great. How'd you know I wasn't working?"

"I actually popped by Rosewood to introduce myself. Dr. Conlan told me you were off tonight."

So he was checking up on me. Fantastic.

I lead him to the sofa in the living room, offering him a seat. He sits, his back straight, his hands carefully positioned on his knees. He looks uncomfortable— then again, I haven't known him to look comfortable.

"Can I get you a drink?" I ask.

"No, I'm fine. I just wanted to see how things are going. How's residency?"

"Great, Dad."

"You know, I was surprised Dr. Conlan said you had the night off. Alex, you're trying to make a good impression here. You should be at the hospital every second you can. During my residency—"

I interrupt. "You never took a single day off. I know, Dad. You've told me."

"It's true. I didn't take a day off. Alex, this is your work. This is your dream. You need to commit."

"And I am. I'm giving it my all." I feel the frustration rising, but try to tell myself to keep it at bay. Dad means well. And even if he doesn't, it's just a few hours. I just have to make it through a few hours.

"Are you still seeing that girl, Alex?"

"Marley? Yes. Did Mom tell you?" I'd been talking

163

about her to Mom the last few times I called. In truth, Marley's basically consumed my thoughts. She's all I talk about.

"She did. I don't think it's a great idea, you know."

"Dad. Listen. I'm doing a good job at the hospital. I don't think it hurts to have some fun outside of work. I'm building a life here, too."

"I don't want you getting distracted."

"I don't think getting distracted is all bad. I have to live a little, too, Dad."

"Living a little leads to sloppy work. This is your career you're building, your reputation. I don't want you wasting your time on some late-summer fling." His judging gaze pierces through me, and I feel the threat of disappointment creep in.

But I'm not the teenage Alex who would do anything just to get a nod from Dad. I love him and I respect him, but this is my life. I need to make my own way.

"She's not a fling. I love her," I spew, anger now bubbling.

"Watch your tone with me, Alex. You better watch your tone. You need to get it together, get over this."

"Or what, Dad?"

"Or maybe you'll be seeing less help. Financially and career-wise. Not everyone has the connections I do. Not everyone leaves residency primed for a top-notch position."

"You know what, Dad, maybe I don't want it. Thanks, but no thanks. I'm building a life here, and

I'm happy. Did you ever think California was your idea and not mine? Did you ever think I had something else in mind?"

His cold stare appraises me. Our gazes are locked, and a chilling silence seeps between us. Finally, he speaks up, enunciating his words as if the pointed quality will make them stick. "You're being an idiot, son. You're better than this."

"Why, Dad? Because I have a different idea for my life than you?"

"What's happened to you? You're falling apart, Alex," Dad spews, rising from his seat, the vein in his forehead popping out.

"What's happened? I've found out there's more to life than what you put on me. I've found my own way. I've found there are other things than work."

"Well, don't come crying to me when it blows up in your face."

"I won't."

We sulk in a screamingly silent moment, both brooding over the newfound tension between us. Maybe it's getting away from home, or maybe it's finding Marley, but suddenly, I see a new side of Dad I didn't see before. I see the side that's worried about success and appearances, not truly about my happiness.

We bridge the gap with discussions of new medical research, the weather, and Mom. When he leaves for the airport, there is a simple, two-slap hug goodbye, and he's gone, not another word spoken.

I sink into the couch for a long moment, the tension still cutting through the air, the knowledge that traveling a slightly different path isn't something my dad will approve of gripping me more than I'd like.

***

I thought my fight with Dad would be the worst part of my night, the worst part of my week. I was irrevocably wrong.

The next night, our fight is a distant memory, one I would go back and relive gladly.

I sit in the middle of the sofa, stretched out, barely remembering how I got here. The past few hours are a fog, but they're also crystal clear. They keep replaying in my head, over and over, nightmare fuel of the worst kind—the real kind.

I'm still wearing my scrubs, the thought of a shower too painful to even consider right now. I sit, surrounded by the smell of the hospital that seeped into me, the lights off.

Surrounded by the smell of death, of regret, of failure.

It's eleven, way earlier than I should be home from the night shift. Dr. Conlan, though, sent me home. There was no argument from me. There was no way I could stay another minute.

My career is over. I'm done.

And worst of all, I think Dad may have been right.

I've lost my focus… and someone else had to pay the price for that.

Chapter Seventeen

Alex

I wake up, still slumped onto the sofa, my neck throbbing, as someone pounds on the door. Light streams through the windows. I groan, feeling hungover even though I haven't had a drop. It takes everything in me to stomp to the door. It's probably Dr. Conlan coming to impart more words of wisdom, to reassure me like he did last night.

But it won't. A family is without their father, their grandfather, their husband, their brother. It's my fault. If I had been more focused, if I had tried harder, this wouldn't have happened.

It's all my fault.

I turn the doorknob, vision blurred from the remnants of a few hours of sleep.

It's not Dr. Conlan, though.

It's Marley.

She leaps through the door, wrapping her arms

around me. I want to tell her to take a step back, that I haven't showered, but once her arms are around my neck, I can't. I fold into her, burying my head in her shoulder.

I'm selfish right now. I can't push her away, even though I should. I can't tell her the "I'm fine" lie, and I can't feel guilty for loving her, despite my dad's warning.

Because right now, holding her is what I need.

"Hey, it's okay, Alex. It's okay. Dr. Conlan called me to tell me what happened." She whispers her words as if she's afraid speaking too loudly might break me. It just might. I've never felt this low, this messed up.

"I fucked up, Marley. It was my fault."

"Shh, no. No, it wasn't. You tried to help him. You tried to save him, you did. Dr. Conlan told me you did all the right things. You did everything right, Alex."

"He died, Marley. He died right in front of me, and I was powerless. I couldn't save him. I didn't save him," I murmur, trying to shove back the tears that want to fall right now, trying to be strong. I grit my teeth, clenching my jaw and exhaling.

"Come on, let's sit down," Marley says, leading me to my sofa.

I slink into the sofa, burying my head in my hands. "I should've been able to save him."

"Hey, look at me," she commands, putting a gentle hand under my chin, pulling my arms away from my face, and turning my head to look at her. I

169

stare into those eyes I've stared into so many times. I feel steadied. I feel grounded in reality. "You can't save everyone, Alex. You can't. It was Mr. Bronson's time. It was his time, you couldn't stop it. Dr. Conlan wouldn't have been able to stop it."

"Yeah, he would. He would've done better. If he wasn't so damn tied up with the car accident victim, he'd have saved him. Or someone else. If someone else had been in my position, maybe Mr. Bronson would've lived. I should've known right away to check for internal bleeding. I should've checked quicker."

She pulls me to her. The tears don't flow. Now, the secondary emotion is building. I'm pissed.

Pissed at myself. Pissed at the situation. Pissed he had to die, pissed Dad is going to see this as a sign he's right, that Marley's distracted me.

And pissed maybe he is right in some ways.

"Listen, Alex. You're a great doctor. Seriously. Dr. Conlan is tough on his staff, but he sings your praises every chance he gets. I know it must be hard to have what happened take place tonight. I know this is your first one. Joe told me he still remembers his first loss. It's not easy, I know. But Alex, think of how many people you've saved. Think about how many you *will* save."

My breathing steadies. "But I should have saved him."

"Alex, you can't be perfect. You're not perfect. No one is. None of us are God. But just because you're not perfect doesn't mean you've failed. You did everything you were supposed to. It was just an unexpected tragedy, an unforeseen side effect. So stop beating yourself up. It's okay to be sad about it. But it's not okay to blame yourself. It's not okay to tell yourself it's your fault. And it's not okay for you to give up on your dreams. You deserve this. You're amazing."

"I let someone die tonight, Marley. He died in front of me." The words keep sticking in my head, repeating themselves over and over.

"But you also have helped so many people live. Like me. You saved me. You saved countless others. You need to stop focusing on your shortcomings and focus on what you've done. Alex, it's like you told me. You deserve to find your happiness. You deserve to give yourself some credit. You're doing a damn good job. Stop holding yourself to perfection. You can be a good doctor and let yourself live a little. And living means you're going to make mistakes. You're not going to be perfect. You have to get used to it. You have to learn to do the best you can and realize it's good enough."

I stare at her, still feeling guilty. I still feel like I failed, and I still feel like shit.

But, for the first time in my life, I also feel accepted for who I am. Not for who I might be. Not for the prestige I can earn, and not for the grades I get on my tests. I feel accepted for who Alex Evans really is, the good and bad. In her eyes, I see acceptance. I see a woman who will stand beside me, who will lift me up when I want to give up. I see a partner. I see a friend. I see a motivation to keep going when things get tough.

I lost someone tonight, and that is awful. I know I'll never forget this night, and I'll never forget his name. I'll never forget the helplessness I felt when he started slipping without warning. I'll never forget the final look on his face or the look on his loved ones' faces when we had to tell them the news.

I know, too, though, I'll never forget this moment right here, how even at my lowest of low moments, her expression, her words, her eyes brought me back. I'll never forget the trust and support I see on her face right now.

I'll never forget the knowledge that Dad is completely wrong.

Marley hasn't distracted me from my dreams. She hasn't forced me to lose focus.

She's done the opposite. She's given me permission to chase my real dreams, and she's given me the motivation to find happiness in this crazy life. She's given purpose to my dreams.

Sitting here with her, I realize before Marley, I was doing all of this as my life. Now, I'm doing all this to build a life with her, to find happiness with her.

I'm not doing it for prestige or success. I'm doing it because being a doctor, being with Marley, they're part of a collective dream I have now. They go hand in hand. This job is brutal and heartbreaking. It's emotionally draining. But with Marley, I feel like it's possible to find happiness in it and outside of it. I feel like I can find balance.

"I love you," I say, leaning in to kiss her on the cheek. "Thank you. I think need to go get a shower."

"I'll make you something to eat," she responds with a smile.

"What about work? Do you have to be up early tomorrow?" I ask, glancing at the time on my phone.

"I called off. This is more important. I'm here for you, Alex. We're here for each other, you know?"

I smile. "You betcha," I say, heading to the shower, my feet a little less heavy.

Chapter Eighteen

Alex

A few weeks later, and I'm mostly back to myself, thanks to Marley and Doctor Conlan. The guilt has eased. I realized when I signed up for this career that loss was a part of the job.

Still doesn't make it easy.

Sitting at the dining room table with Margaret, Joe, and Marley, I smile as I reach for my wineglass. It's easy to see how much they love Marley.

It's easy to see how anyone could.

Marley's mom, Jolene, was invited tonight, of course, but she couldn't make it. She had a date with some guy named Bill who Marley insists is bad news but didn't really want to talk about.

She seems okay, though. I think at this point, as sad as it is, Marley knows she can't count on her mom.

But she still feels the need to protect her.

"I'm stuffed, Mrs. Conlan. That was the best roast

beef I've ever had," I say.

"That's because you're used to eating Doritos and energy drinks," Marley chimes in.

Margaret points a finger at me. "That's terrible. You come over anytime. Joe, you should have told me this poor boy needs a home-cooked meal. I'd have invited him over sooner."

Joe smiles. "Well, dear, to do that, these two lovebirds would have to make time to pop by instead of going out and doing whatever the young kids are doing these days."

Marley smiles. "Oh, stop. You know we love hanging with you two."

"Yeah, Joe. Speak for yourself. I'm young and hip still," Margaret asserts, winking at us.

She reaches over to pat Marley's arm. "Will you come help me in the kitchen? I made some cookies, but I want to get them onto trays."

"Sure thing," Marley replies, turning to smile at me before following Margaret. Smoky rubs my leg and I reach down to pet the purring cat as the two women scurry off to the other room, talking and laughing about something on their way.

Joe, sitting across from me, props his elbows on the table and folds his hands.

"You two are so good for each other." He says it pointedly but with a grin. He declares it like he's giving approval. Maybe he is.

"My dad seems to think she's distracting me." The

words slip off my tongue. There's something about Joe that makes me want to confide in him. I suppose it's from our time together at the hospital. Another part of it is that he's almost become like the dad I don't have. A kind, empathetic one who is always perceptive to what I need.

"Son, I think she's grounding you. Being a doctor isn't easy. You need someone who will keep you in check with real life. Marley will do that."

"How do you know?"

"Because I see so much of my Margaret in her. Margaret's the one who has kept me going, who has kept me wanting to do this job. I'm telling you, if you make this your life, you're going to burn out. You're going to wake up and wonder what it was all for. Keep that girl close. You're good for each other."

I smile, knowing he's right.

"I just… I want to help her. I know she wants more than Georgia's."

"I've been wanting more for her this whole time. I know why she won't go to college. I know why she didn't leave here. Margaret and I tried to tell her we'd watch over her mom, that we'd help her. But she won't leave. I think she feels guilty. I think she just needs someone, the right someone, to give her a little shove," Joe says, winking at me.

"I don't know how."

"You're a smart guy. You'll figure it out." He reaches for his wineglass now, giving me a wink and a nod.

"What are you two talking about?" Marley asks, coming back to the dining room with a serving tray of cookies.

"Just life," Joe responds.

Marley raises an eyebrow, looking between us. "Sounds... interesting."

"I hope so," Joe agrees cryptically, and Marley just shakes her head, urging everyone to take a cookie as we settle in for more stories, more laughter, and more realizations this is what life is all about.

Chapter Nineteen

Marley

Finishing my latest poem during break, I close the pages of my journal as I scurry back inside to help Louise. The weather is chilling, but I still like to sit in my spot. It's where I get my writing mojo. Ever since the night Alex made me share my poetry, my journal's now busting with poems about so many different things.

And the best news? I actually like them. I actually can see them in a poetry collection someday, my name on the cover.

I've been back to Delilah's once, Alex by my side, to share another poem. The thing is, getting up at the mic this time, I wasn't shaking. I wasn't terrified.

I was excited.

I scurry back inside, Louise waiting on a single customer on this humdrum Tuesday in November. The kids are busy in school, the college kids are gone, and the sleepy town of Rosewood is even sleepier, if that's possible.

Luckily, though, I have a hot doctor to fill my nights and, when he snags a day off, my days, too. We've been exploring Rosewood's offerings, both places we've been and places Alex hasn't tried. We've been branching out, though, too. He took me to a museum a few hours away a couple of weeks ago, and I surprised him with a trip to a zoo just a few towns over. We've been exploring, reimagining our lives, and growing together.

Even though things with Mom are still far from perfect, I'm getting a glimpse of what happiness could mean with Alex.

It's hard, though, to let myself become completely invested. Because in a few short years, he'll be done here. And I guess I'm just a little afraid I'll be left in the shadows, wondering what I'm going to do next.

As if he knew I was thinking about him, he comes wandering through the door, an excited look on his face.

"Hey, come with me," he says animatedly, as I reach to pour him a coffee.

"I'm working, though."

"No, you're not. You're the one playing hooky today." He grins, and I raise an eyebrow.

"I think we're a bad influence on each other," I admit, turning to Louise.

"Go ahead, sweetie. Alex already gave Dane a

heads-up. You're free to go. Get out of this place. Have some fun for me while you're at it." She lets out a little chuckle that would be mildly off-putting, but I'm too elated to think about it. I toss my apron in the back, quickly pour a cup of coffee to-go for Alex, and follow him out into the chilling day, ready to see what adventure he has in store for us.

***

Alex leads me to my spot, the oak tree, the one I showed him one time—and yes, things got a little spicy under the branches of the oak, which is luckily in a pretty secluded spot.

"So are you going for a replay?" I ask, leaning on his arm.

"No. Yes. Not exactly," he replies, hands in his pockets as we stroll toward the big, sturdy trunk. "Let's sit."

I do as he asks, both of us sitting cross-legged in the grass. I pick at a blade of grass, smiling at Alex, wondering what we're doing.

"I have something for you," he says mysteriously, and he reaches into his pocket to pull something out.

"What is it?" I ask, confused as he hands me some papers. He brought me to this tree to give me some junk mail? Some brochures? What's going on? Is he delirious?

"Read it," he commands.

I bite my lip as I unfold the papers, not sure what to

expect in the least.

But when I open it, I'm more confused.

It's a pamphlet for a writing program at Queens University in Charlotte.

As in North Carolina. As in several hours away.

"Okay. I don't understand."

Alex's face turns into a huge grin as he looks at me pointedly. "Well, they have a great creative writing program. It's amazing, and it'll help you get your poetry going."

"Alex, I can't. This is in North Carolina."

"Exactly. It's out of Rosewood. It's away from here. A new place to explore, a new path. It'll be great."

I look at him like he's just suggested the earth is flat or that Keith Urban just agreed to marry me.

"They won't accept me. I had terrible grades."

"But they will. I've been in contact with them. I explained your poetry writing. I talked to them about your credentials. The admissions counselor wants to meet with you, wants to see your work."

I stare at him, trying to remind myself to keep my mouth closed. "You did what?"

"I'm sorry. I know. I should've told you. But I knew you needed a little push. I know you want more in life, Marley, and I know you want to pursue your writing. I also knew you'd never give yourself permission to pursue it."

"So you just did it for me?" I ask, a little taken aback. I'm shocked. I'm confused. I'm floored he did this.

"Are you mad?" he asks gingerly, apparently the thought crossing his mind for the first time.

I take a second to reexamine the blade of grass, taking a deep breath. "No." I look up at him. "I'm just scared. North Carolina's pretty far from here. I don't know."

"But Marley, it's only about five hours. Five hours to make a start for yourself, to do something just for you. I know you worry about your mom, but I've already talked to Joe and Margaret. They'll watch out for her. You know they will. And I'll be here."

"That's part of the problem, too. You'll be *here*. I'll be there. This will never work."

He reaches for my hands, forcing me to drop the blade of grass. "Of course it will. I'll come see you. You'll come see me. We'll talk. It's just for a few years. I love you. Trust in that. Don't let the fear of losing me, of losing anyone, stop you. You need to do this for you."

I look at him, at the faith he has in me, and I tear up.

I want to be the brave Marley I try to be, the front I put out there. I want my adventurous parts of life to be about more than jumping in a mud puddle or taking a selfie in the rain. I want to explore this world, to get out there, to find myself. I want to laugh and cry. I want to be scared. I want to scare someone. I want to travel, to learn, to reach, to find, and to run. I want to do everything with someone else. I want to be with someone through it all, to experience what life has to offer with no regrets.

Above all, I want to do this with the man who rescued me and the man who has inspired me to be something more. I want to do all of this with the straitlaced-turned-somewhat-spontaneous man who makes me feel like life and love are possible.

I want to find my way with Alex. I want every piece of me to be his, in every way.

But I don't know if I can. Because the thought of it all is more than just a little scary. It's guilt-ridden. It's complicated. Am I ready to move on? Can I leave this place behind?

Can I leave Mom behind?

I know it's crazy. There have been so many times when I wasn't her priority. There are so many in town who whisper I'm nuts or that I'm an angel for sticking around. I'm neither.

I'm just the little girl who cried in the backyard as her mother crumpled to the ground with the news her daddy was dead. I'm the little girl who worried her mom was going to die too if she didn't stop crying in her bedroom.

I'm the seven-year-old who lived with the Conlans for a summer while Mom got help.

I'm the eight-year-old who didn't want to tell anyone Mom wasn't doing better, that she was gone more than she was home, and that even when she was home, she spent so much time drinking from the bottle that she wasn't helpful anyway.

I'm the sixteen-year-old Marley who said screw it and gave up on finding a way out, on a new happiness, and on things every being okay.

I'm the eighteen-year-old Marley who packed up her stuff to leave, but turned right around at the sight of her mom crying, begging me not to leave, too.

I'm the twenty-one-year-old Marley who is ready to live life but feels like doing so would be abandoning her mom. I feel like I'd be letting Dad down. I couldn't save him when I was seven, but I can save Mom. I can save her from herself, from complete destruction, and from giving up.

I can be here to support her. I can take care of her.

I have to take care of her.

I don't shoot down the idea right away, though. It's too painful to just let it slip from my hands so quickly, just like everything else.

"I'll think about it," I say, mostly to placate him as well as the woman inside of me begging for escape. He leans in to kiss my cheek, the pamphlet still in my hand, the branches of the oak fanning above us as a few raindrops fall down.

Chapter Twenty

Marley

Later that night, back at my house, I sit in my room. The lamp is on, the pamphlet gleaming underneath it on the nightstand. I stare at the bright, crisp cover, two students ambling on the campus. For a moment, I picture myself there.

I picture myself taking writing classes, working toward my goal. I picture myself out of Georgia's, living life, going somewhere.

But could I do it? Could I leave this place?

Could I leave Mom behind?

I know it's crazy. Most twenty-one-year-olds are long gone by now, loosed from the confines of their parents. I know, too, that sometimes Mom doesn't deserve so much consideration. God knows she doesn't give it to me.

I just can't feel good, completely good, about leaving, though. What if it's the final straw? What if she completely breaks? How would I live with that?

Then again, is it fair for me to be here forever, tied to a stagnant life, tied to the anvil in the river at Cedar Bend Bridge? Is it fair my life stopped when my dad made his choice? Is it fair to keep myself from happiness forever?

I bury my head in a pillow, muffling my scream. Life is too hard. Even now, with Alex in my life, things are so hard.

There is no easy answer.

I lie awake in bed all night, thinking about my future, about life, about Alex. I try to figure out how to solve this.

When the alarm rings in the morning, though, and I realize I fell asleep somewhere between my two options, I groggily get out of bed, carrying the pamphlets out to the kitchen, tossing them in the trash.

Who am I kidding? Who do I think I am? I'm not college material. I'm not poetry material. Most of all, I'm not leaving material.

I trudge off to my routine, to my life, to my forever planted here in the small town I'll never escape.

***

Alex is working tonight, so after my shift, I head straight home for a shower and some television. I startle when I walk through the door and find Mom on the couch.

"Mom. I thought you'd still be sleeping." In truth, this is all Mom seems to do lately. Work, Bill, or sleep.

I've barely seen her, for better or worse.

"Marley, sit." Mom motions toward the empty chair. She is silent and stoic, remarkably calm. She seems peaceful, her hair not the frizzy mess it usually is. She's wearing jeans and a solid blue top. She looks pretty. She looks like a snapshot of the Mom I once knew.

"Marley, I know I've been a shit mom."

I open my mouth to stop her, waving my hand. She puts her hand up to shush me.

"Stop. Listen. I know I've messed up. Big time. I've never gotten myself together for you. I haven't been there. I certainly have my reasons, but that doesn't mean I have a good excuse. Time and time again, I've let you down. I've fallen into bad cycles. I don't think I'll ever be the mom you deserve. Truly. I know that."

"Mom, I love you. Stop."

"I love you too, Marley. Which is why, for once in my life, I need to do the right thing. I need you to do the right thing." She reaches behind her, pulling out the crumpled brochures. "You need to go."

"Mom, those are nothing."

"Stop it. I found them in the trash while Margaret and Joe were here. I know what they mean. Margaret, Joe, and I had a long, long talk. They made me see some things I've been too selfish to see. I see it now. And I'm telling you to go."

I freeze, stunned by her words, by the thought of Joe and Margaret talking about this with her. Most of all, I'm stunned by the thought of her listening, of her taking it to heart. Still, this can't be right. This can't be. I shake my head, dismissing the conversation, saying, "I don't want to. It was stupid, really."

"Listen to me. I may be a drunk and a bad mom, but I'm not an idiot. I know living here isn't what you want. I've just been too selfish to let you go. And you're too good of a person to leave. But stop using me as an excuse. Stop being afraid to fail or to mess up. Go, Marley. Go. See what life has for you. Staying here isn't going to change me. My cards have been played. I've made my choices. But I can have some satisfaction in the thought your life isn't completely fucked-up. You can still find a good life. So you need to go. It's not a question. It's an order."

Tears are streaming down my face. For the first time in a long time, I see a hint of who Mom is, who Mom could've been.

I see an unselfish woman who just wants the best for me. I see love. I see a desire for me to succeed.

Without a word, I do something I haven't in a while. I traipse across the room, sit on the couch beside her, and fall into her arms, tears streaming.

"I'm scared," I cry into her shoulder, feeling again like the eight-year-old girl. This time, though, Mom is there to be a mom, to hold me, to tell me it's going to be okay.

"You're going to soar, Marley. Let me let you soar."

And suddenly, I know Alex has done me one better

than rescuing me from the bridge.

He's helped me rescue myself. He's helped Mom rescue us.

He's saved my present, my future, and my dreams.

Chapter Twenty-One

Alex

Her hair is billowing behind her as the November sun grazes across her skin. She clings to my arm like she has so many other times as we walk through Rosewood after a long day of work for both of us.

The thing is, though, where I used to be apt to stay at work, to bask in the glow of my accomplishments, I'm now looking forward to these moments. Work is only one part of me.

Marley's the other.

We stroll down the sidewalk, and I veer left, taking us to what's quickly become our spot.

"So what time are your parents coming tomorrow?" she asks.

"I think ten."

"Perfect. Joe and Margaret are planning dinner for noon. Will that be enough time?"

"Of course. I can't wait for Mom and Dad to meet you."

She bites her lip. "You sure they're ready for that? You sure you're ready?"

"Marley, we've been through this. They're going to love you."

"Are they going to love all of me though? As in, my family, too?"

I smile. "Of course. They'll love you because how could they not? You're amazing."

Thanksgiving dinner is going to be at the Conlans' place tomorrow. Margaret's already busy working on the pies. They were gracious to extend the invite to me this year and to my folks. Even Marley's mom is going to come this year. It's going to be a big bash.

And I truly do believe my parents are going to love her. My dad's certainly not over his fears of Marley distracting me or the fact he thinks I'm making mistakes. He still hasn't let go of the fantasy that I'll return home, the perfect son, ready to live out his version of my dreams. We've still got a lot of progress to do.

Still, I know at the end of it, it's my life and my decision. I also know that Marley is amazing. I think some time with her will convince my dad I'm not totally lost—but we'll just have to see. As Marley's taught me, we can't control our families. We can only control our own happiness, and I'm taking the reins of mine, whether my dad agrees with me or not.

"This will be Mom's first year at Thanksgiving in a while. She never would come with me. Dad always loved the holiday and, truth be told, I don't know if Mom felt like she had much to be thankful for."

"Well," I say as we get to the middle of the bridge, to the exact spot, "I have a lot to be thankful for this year." I lean in and kiss her against the banister, the breeze blowing against my back.

She pulls back slightly, grinning. "Careful, doctor boy. You wouldn't want to have to jump in again for me. I think the water might be a bit colder this time of year."

I eye her seriously, the girl with raven-black hair who stole every piece of me right here from the moment I first saw her.

"I'd jump in that water a hundred times for you. Seriously."

"I know you would. And I love you for it. But how about we stay up here for today? I'm okay with not being rescued, at least physically." She puts a hand on my jaw and pulls me back in. We kiss for a long while.

"What are you going to do without me?" she asks, and I grin weakly.

It's a thought that's been crossing my mind more than sporadically these days.

In a month, she leaves for North Carolina, her acceptance official. She'll be gone from this place, finally spreading her wings, and I'll be left behind.

It's an odd sensation.

"I'll miss the hell out of you. But we'll make up for it when I get to see you," I reply, and she nuzzles into me.

"You betcha," she says.

I pull back. "You betcha."

And it's true. I'm going to miss her like crazy. I'm going to miss our easy routines, our walks together through the tiny town. I'm going to miss seeing her smile every day and her crazy adventures. I'm going to miss all of her.

But I'm happy as hell, too. I'm thrilled to see her thrive in this new chapter of life. I'm ecstatic she's getting out of here and chasing her dreams. I'm happy to see the sadness of the girl on the ledge of the bridge that night has faded away and, in its place, this Marley has surfaced. The Marley I think she always wanted to be.

That's the thing about that night. Neither of us knew what was coming with that slip, with that tumble down, down into the water. Neither of us could've predicted how much a fall would change both of us.

But change us it did.

Because as much as Marley's surfaced and been freed from her past, so have I. I'm a new version of Alex Evans. I'm a freer man, a man with a life he's looking forward to living.

Marley helped me raise my head and look around me. She helped me see not just the ultimate goal, but the views along the way. She helped me see life not just as a job but as a possibility, as excitement, as real life.

And, standing here, looking at the view from the

193

Cedar Bend Bridge, I know I can't even begin to imagine where this life with her is going to take me.

"I'm scared to leave, Alex. But you know what? I'm also not. Because I know, no matter what, you'll be here, ready to save me if I need it."

I kiss her cheek. "I will. And I know the same thing about you."

"Maybe falling from the ledge wasn't such a bad thing after all, you know?" She smiles at me, readjusting her blue hat—she's switched colors in preparation for her college days, deciding blue looked more poet-like.

She looks into my eyes, the mysterious woman I've been unwrapping these past few months, the woman I've come to love more than anything.

Looking out at the view from the bridge, glancing toward the horizon, I smile. "Maybe not. Maybe not at all," I say, Marley leaning on my arm as we stare off into the distance, ready for whatever is up ahead.

Epilogue

Alex

Two and a half years later

It's finished.

I can hardly believe my time is done, and the coat is officially, completely mine.

Dr. Evans. It's something I've worked so hard to earn, to completely earn. And now that residency's finished, I feel I've put the last brick in the wall, in the foundation for my future.

I'm free to take the next step.

And take the next step I am… today.

When I came to Rosewood, love wasn't important to me. Living a free, adventurous life wasn't important. Only the feel of the coat on my body, the rush of saving lives, and the pull of my endless shifts mattered. The thought of climbing the ladder, of getting back to California to the prestigious hospital Dad picked out mattered. I would carry on the family tradition and chase the family dream without stopping to smell the roses or take in anything along the way.

Now, though, so much has changed. Standing at the bridge where it all shifted, even if I didn't know it quite then, I take a deep breath.

Everything has changed in the past few years, but one thing has stayed constant.

Marley. Even miles and miles away, she's still managed to permeate my life. A single conversation with her, a single word, a single look is all I need. She reminds me life is about living, about going out and exploring.

She saved me from myself, from my family, and from a life I couldn't possibly want.

The California dreams that were never really mine are long gone. I've applied for and accepted a position in a North Carolina hospital that lacks the prestige but has one very crucial benefit California doesn't: Marley.

She's got another year and a half of school before it's off to new adventures. College is suiting her well, and she's already had a few of her poems published. The sky is the limit, and I have no idea where life's taking her. The good news is, doctors are everywhere, so my possibilities are also endless.

Margaret and Joe couldn't be prouder, and Jolene too. She's actually started a new job as an administrative assistant at the hospital thanks to Joe, and things are going well. She's got a new boyfriend, a construction worker a town over, who seems like a decent guy. She's not perfect, and she still has her moments. She still falls from time to time.

But the thing I've come to realize is—don't we all? Don't we all need saving? Whether it's the pull of the bottle or the pull of morose feelings or the pull of perfectionist tendencies, sometimes we all need someone to save us from our worst enemy: ourselves.

And, thankfully, I've found that here in Rosewood, not just in Marley, but in Joe, in Margaret, and even in Jolene. We've become a ragtag family and, in many ways, they've filled a void my own family never could.

I didn't come to Rosewood for love. I came here thinking it'd be a temporary stop on the way to a lifetime of success. Now, though, I realize I'm not the same Alex Evans I was when I got here, and I'm more than okay with that.

Now, I'm ready to take the next wild and free step with her, a step I never thought possible when I came here.

So, as we stand in that spot, our spot, I turn to her, her warm hands resting in mine, and I begin my carefully planned words as she stares up at me.

"I love you, Marley Jade. From the moment I was lucky enough to spot you on this bridge, from the first words you said to me, I've loved you. All of you. I love the way you dance in the rain and take me on crazy hikes. I love how you make me want to explore, to be, to just live. When I got here, I thought I had my life all mapped out. I thought I was doing it all right. But then you came along, and you awakened me. You made me realize I had no idea what I was doing before you. I was lost, Marley. I was drowning in a life I didn't exactly understand. You helped me see through the murky waters and find my way. Two of us got saved that night. Two of us. And I think together, we can keep saving each other. Let me be the man who saves you when you need help, and who lets you fly when you're feeling strong. Let me be the man beside you in every step. Let me be the man to explore this crazy thing called life, no matter where it takes you. I love you."

Tears are flowing now, her black hair billowing in the gentle breeze like it did that August night when I first saw her. Standing at the spot where she almost disappeared and where my life changed forever, I drop to one knee, and she gasps, the chatty girl at a loss for words. She puts one hand on her beloved hat, clutching it as if she's clinging to life, as if she knows everything's going to change.

And I hope to hell it is. I hope this is the moment that takes us into the next chapter.

"I love you, with everything I am, and with everything I hope to be. I don't know exactly where we're going. I don't know the details of where this life is going to end up, but you've taught me that's okay. That's more than okay. That's the way it's supposed to be. You make me want to be free, Marley. You make me want to live. Let me be the one who walks this crazy path with you. Let me be the one who can smile with you, laugh with you, and cry with you when we need to. Let me love all of you. Marry me." I look up at the woman who changed everything. I look up and see the woman who made me realize I was so much more than a list of expectations. I look up at the woman who reintroduced me to Alex Evans and to who I want to be.

I see the woman who makes every breath, every hardship, everything worthwhile.

My heart flutters just like it did the first night when my foot slammed on the brakes. We're at another pivotal point, a moment that feels like life or death.

Because if she says no, it will in many ways be the death of me.

Marley stares at me as I clutch her hands, my breath not coming.

There is a pregnant pause, an interminable silence.

And then, her pink lips spread into a huge smile. "You betcha, doctor boy."

She sinks to her knees right there, and we kiss each other with a fire we've come to know in each other. Like two crazy people, we make out right there by the side of the bridge where we almost lost it all and where we found it all. When we finally pull back, clinging to each other, I reach into my pocket.

"I almost forgot," I say, pulling out the ring box.

I pop it open, and she smiles as the bright yellow diamond gleams at her.

"It's gorgeous," she exclaims, putting her hands over her face.

"Look inside," I whisper, and she carefully pulls out the ring from the box.

Engraved inside is: "All of you."

"I want you to know," I say, "that no matter what happens, I'll love you. All of you. Forever. There's nothing you could do to make me love you less."

She laughs as I slide the ring onto her hand. "It's perfect. It's absolutely perfect. I love you," she says through her tears. My heart pangs at the sight of the ring on her left hand, at the thought we're starting our next chapter together.

We kiss again before standing and looking out over the Cedar Bend Bridge, admiring the sunset from a safe distance.

"You ready for whatever's next?" I ask, squeezing her hand that now has my ring on it.

She leans into me, squeezing my arm. "You betcha," she answers, and we head off into the great unknown together, walking away from the bridge and toward a new horizon.

Acknowledgements

First and foremost, I want to thank my amazing publisher, Hot Tree Publishing. Thank you, Becky, for believing in my writing and in my dreams. Your dedication to your authors, readers, and the beauty of the romance genre is so motivating. Thank you for giving me such a wonderful place to call home as a writer. Thank you to Liv, Justine, Claire, Peggy, Donna, and everyone else who works tirelessly to make sure every story is the best version it can be. Thank you to the authors at Hot Tree Publishing for being such an amazing, inspirational team.

Thank you to my parents, Ken and Lori Keagy, for always supporting me in my dreams. Thank you for teaching me to love books, writing, and to be confident in my goals. I love you both so much.

Thanks to my husband, Chad, for holding my hand on this writing journey. You're always there to motivate me to keep going. I am so lucky to have married my absolute best friend.

Thank you to my friends, family, and coworkers who support my writing in so many ways. Thank you, Grandma Bonnie, for always being at all my events and for always being one of the first to get a copy of every book. Thank you to my in-laws, Tom and Diane, for always being so supportive. Thank you to Christie James, Kristin Mathias, Kristin Books, Jamie Lynch, Lynette Luke, Jennifer Carney, Alicia Schmouder, Kelly Rubritz, Heather Jasinski, Deborah Biter, and everyone else who supports my writing dreams. I am so lucky to have so many amazing people encouraging me to keep going and to keep writing.

Thank you to Kay Shuma for following me from day one and always encouraging me to keep telling my stories. Your support is amazing and an inspiration.

Thank you to my local Barnes & Noble and Bradley's Book Outlet for supporting local authors like me. A special thank-you goes out to Lisa Sprankle and Jennifer Lilly for always opening your doors to me for author events.

Thank you to all of the book bloggers who tirelessly help promote writers like me. Thank you to all of my readers for helping me pursue my writing dreams. Your support means everything.

Finally, a thank-you goes to my best friend, Henry, for always being there to make me smile. I will never have enough time with you or enough cupcakes with you. Thanks for reminding me what unconditional love looks like and for showing me that sometimes the best things in life come along when you least expect them.

About the Author

A high school English teacher, an author, and a fan of anything pink and/or glittery, Lindsay's the English teacher cliché; she loves cats, reading, Shakespeare, and Poe.

She currently lives in her hometown with her husband, Chad (her junior high sweetheart); their cats, Arya, Amelia, Alice, and Bob; and their Mastiff, Henry.

Lindsay's goal with her writing is to show the power of love and the beauty of life while also instilling a true sense of realism in her work. Some reviewers have noted that her books are not the "typical romance." With her novels coming from a place of honesty, Lindsay examines the difficult questions, looks at the tough emotions, and paints the pictures that are sometimes difficult to look at. She wants her fiction to resonate with readers as realistic, poetic, and powerful. Lindsay wants women readers to be able to say, "I see myself in that novel." She wants to speak to the modern woman's experience while also bringing a twist of something new and exciting. Her aim is for readers to say, "That could happen," or "I feel like the characters are real." That's how she knows she's done her job.

Lindsay's hope is that by becoming a published author, she can inspire some of her students and other aspiring writers to pursue their own passions. She wants them to see that any dream can be attained and publishing a novel isn't out of the realm of possibility.

Lindsay loves connecting with readers. She'd love for you to reach out to her.

WEBSITE: WWW.LINDSAYDETWILER.COM
TWITTER: TWITTER.COM/LINDSAYDETWILER
INSTAGRAM: INSTAGRAM.COM/LINDSAYANNDETWILER
FACEBOOK:FACEBOOK.COM/LINDSAYANNDETWILER
NEWSLETTER: HTTP://BIT.LY/2U42BJU

About the Publisher

Hot Tree Publishing opened its doors in 2015 with an aspiration to bring quality fiction to the world of readers. With the initial focus on romance and a wide spread of romance sub-genres, they envision opening up to alternative genres in the near future.

Firmly seated in the industry as a leading editing provider to independent authors and small publishing houses, Hot Tree Publishing is the sister company to Hot Tree Editing, founded in 2012. Having established in-house editing and promotions, plus having a well-respected market presence, Hot Tree Publishing endeavors to be a leader in bringing quality stories to the world of readers.

Interested in discovering more amazing reads brought to you by Hot Tree Publishing? Head over to the website FOR INFORMATION:

WWW.HOTTREEPUBLISHING.COM

CPSIA information can be obtained
at www.ICGtesting.com
Printed in the USA
BVHW01s0143020118
504076BV00001B/1/P